Obsidian Dreams

"The way had not, at all times and places, the selfsame name; the sage had not, at all times and places, the selfsame body. Heaven caused a suitable religion to be instituted for every region and clime so that each one of the races of mankind might be saved."

Emperor Tang Taizong of China

638 AD

Contents

Part 1 - 1989 After the earthquake

Stephen glanced down and noticed waves forming in the glass of tequila he had been sipping. Instinctively he grabbed onto the counter to keep from falling off his stool. Looking up he saw bottles dancing on the shelves across from where he was sitting. Some of them fell to the tile floor. As they broke, Tequila and shards of glass came splashing back up onto the counter. Behind him, people were screaming and running around in chaos. Then, as quickly as it had come, it was over. All that remained was the broken glass, the smell of the spilled tequila and the undefined loud murmur of hundreds of people all excitedly talking at once. He looked up and down the concourse, shook his head and thought about how time seemed to have slowed down. An earthquake is almost like a dream, he thought, all of the solid things we normally take for granted move and shake. Then, when it's over, we are not quite sure what happened.

Before the earthquake, Stephen had been sitting quietly sipping Tequila in a bar at the airport in Mexico City. He was a feature writer for AP. It was the end of a long business trip in Mexico. His current assignment was an article about the aftermath of the 1988 election. The task was to discover hard evidence that the ruling PRI party rigged the election. In the past two weeks he had gathered the facts and was ready to go home and write the finished article.

He finished his tequila, put some money on the counter, got up and tried to avoid the broken glass on the floor as he went over to the gate that his flight had been scheduled to depart from. He discovered that it was cancelled because of problems due to the earthquake. The agent said that there were no more flights until the next day and his luggage would be unloaded and delivered later to his hotel. He booked a new flight, called his wife, and then left a message for his boss. There was nothing else he could do at the airport. So he walked outside and got a cab.

Even though it was a cloudy afternoon, He decided to go downtown and take a walk in a quiet old neighborhood north of the Cathedral on Calle Mina.

A cab ride in Mexico City was always an adventure. But today he didn't look out at the life on the streets as he usually did. He was disappointed not to be going home. Stephen was only fifty years old, but he was thinking of retirement. He loved the challenges of being a writer, especially the challenges of writing about, and understanding Mexico. But he was ready to leave the world of airplanes and hotels, he wanted to spend his time at home writing the novel he had been planning for years and working in his gardens and forest property. He was an avid reader of history. In fact, many years before, he had hoped to become a history teacher. But, as it does to a lot of people, life slapped him in the face and sent him down another path. So here he was, with time on his hands, in one of the most fascinating cities in the world.

He looked up and saw that the cab had just passed the Cathedral and was turning left and would soon stop and drop him off at the Plaza De Santo Domingo.

He had been on Calle Mina and some of the other old streets in the center of the city before. Many of the oldest stone and block buildings were leaning at odd angles. They were not well maintained and little bit decrepit. The paint on almost all the doorways was peeling and cracked, even the cobbled street itself was humped and uneven. It reminded him of the old German impressionist movie "The Cabinet of Doctor Caligari". There were no tidy straight lines, everything was crooked and askew. He was still feeling slightly off balance from the earthquake. This feeling intensified the off kilter and unreal sensation he had as he walked down the street.

The earthquake had damaged some of the buildings. Stone blocks and pieces of concrete that had fallen from a few of the older buildings and were lying in the street. He looked down at one of the pieces of stone. The mortar had broken off and there were fragments of Mexica[1] carvings on the back. He had read several books about the conquest of Mexico. He knew that the Spanish tore down Tenochtitlan[2], filled in the lake the city was built on, and used the stone to build their own city. Building on rubble in an ancient earthquake prone lake bed was, of course, what had caused all the leaning and settling that he saw as he walked down the street. He looked down again and saw a stone that had carving on its face. He picked it up and stood there for a minute or so holding it in his hand, imagining the ancient temples, markets and canals of the Mexica city. He felt a tap on his shoulder and was suddenly brought back to the present by three young people politely telling him to give them the stone. They all wore official lanyards with the logo of the Museo Nacional de Antropologia. His Spanish was very nearly fluent so he spent several minutes talking to them about what they thought the stone might have been. They said they were students and interns and they worked for the Museo. Their project was to assess the scanty archeological evidence indicating that at this exact place the Mexica has

---

[1] This is what the Aztecs called themselves

[2] Tenochtitlan was the name of the capital and center of the Mexica empire. It was located in the center of modern Mexico City. It was built in the middle of a lake. The infrastructure of the city was composed of a network of canals connected to the mainland by long causeways. Before the Spanish arrived the population is estimated to have been between 200 and 300,000, making it one of the biggest cities in the world at that time. Accounts by seasoned and well-traveled Spanish conquistadors tell us that it was the cleanest and most beautiful city they had ever seen.

begun to build a temple to celebrate the accession of the young warrior Tlatoani[3], Cuauhtémoc . This happened in the period between the retreat of the Spanish, which began with what is called the "La Noche Triste[4]" on June 30, 1520, and ended when they returned in August 1521. During the year's respite, the Mexica were decimated by smallpox. New structures were started but never finished. After the conquest, the Spanish used the stones from the Mexica temples and palaces to build their own city. The students told Stephen that the building across from where they were standing may have been built with stones from one of these temples. The Museo students thanked Stephen as he handed them the stone and they carefully wrapped it and stacked it in the back of an official Museo pickup truck along with other stones they had found.

The students drove off and he continued walking. Besides the stone and concrete, there was debris of every kind lying around the old cobbled street, Stephen looked down and noticed something odd in front of him. He picked it up. It was a very old box of head gaskets for 1954 Ford V-8

---

[3] Tlatoani is the title given to the military, political and religious leader of the Mexica.

[4] La Noche Triste (The Night of Sorrows) refers to the Spanish retreat from Tenochtitlan. The population and nobility rose up against the Spanish forcing them to escape at night across one of the causeways leading to the mainland. Historians estimate that 15% to over 50% of the Spanish conquistadors were killed during their escape. Much of the treasure that the Spanish had looted during their stay in the city was lost in the lake.

engines. It is common in this part of Mexico City to find things like this even if there had not been an earthquake. He stood there turning the box over and over in his hands and wondering where it might have come from.

Suddenly he felt something rubbing the back of his legs and turned around to see a very large dog looking up at him. He was startled and jumped back. There was an even larger woman, a black woman, standing there, straining to pull the dog's leash. She was cursing at the dog while smiling at Stephen and mumbling that the dog was a good dog and that the Senor, meaning Stephen, should not worry. The woman, who must have been at least 6 feet tall and probably, weighed over 200 pounds, looked strong. The dog, some sort of mastiff, looked to be about 150 pounds. It had a heavily muscled body and a huge head. The woman was dressed in a tight purple flowered dress. She wore way too much make up. It seemed likely that she was one of the "ladies of the street". She looked at Stephen and said "Tezca wants you to pet his head, go ahead, he seems to like you. He won't bite unless I tell him to." Stephen looked at her, and then down at the slobbering dog, and then down at his hand. He hoped his hand would survive. He reached down and stroked the dog on the head. The dog panted and rubbed up against him again and then rolled over on the ground in the posture that he knew meant that the dog wanted his belly scratched. Stephen loved dogs and this one seemed to be a good dog. So he bent over, talked to the dog and rubbed his belly. After a moment, the woman looked at the gaskets he still held, "That's what I was looking for, they belong to Diego the mechanic. I must have dropped them." She held out her hand and Stephen stood up and handed them to her. She nodded and mumbled "Gracias, bueno dias", cursed again at the dog, pulled him and they began to walk away. Stephen watched as they walked down the uneven cobbled street. The dog kept turning and looking back at him. Every time he turned there were flashes of light reflecting back at Stephen from the odd collar that the dog wore. The dog stopped and scratched his neck with his back leg. Stephen saw something bright fall from his collar. They continued on and Stephen walked over to where they had been. He reached down to pick the object up. It was a small flat black stone, highly polished and reflective on one side. He stood there looking at it and then looked up to call out to the woman. The dog was looking back at him and suddenly there was a loud crack, boom and concussion. He felt as if something heavy had slammed him down and he found himself lying on the street, very shaken and dazed with all kinds of possibilities of disasters sprinting through his brain. After a moment of near panic he realized that he was very wet. Rain was coming down so hard it was stinging his head. The concussion had been a very close lightning strike and accompanying thunder. He immediately got up and ran into an open doorway. As he looked down the street the woman

9

and the dog were disappearing into one of the other buildings.

Doors on the streets of most of these older Mexican neighborhoods usually lead into interior courtyards bordered by more doors. This was the case for the building he had run into. He saw that one of those interiors doors was open. The stone was still in his hand – He stuffed it into his pocket.

An old man stood in the doorway looking at him. "Please come in, get out of the rain"', he said in English. The old man looked about 70. He was medium height and seemed to be trim and fit. His once white, short sleeve shirt had two buttons open at the neck. His unruly hair was still dark. He had a small mustache and looked as if he had not shaved for a few days. Stephen followed him as he walked in to a large room with one bare light bulb hanging from a dark ceiling. There were small windows up high on one side of the room. They let in some light but not enough. The only furniture was a table with two chairs. Another old man was sitting there eating soup. There was a single red rose in a vase on the table. Stephen would have expected a dark old room like this to feel and smell closed and stuffy but the rose was quite splendid and its fragrance permeated the room. The two men looked like either father or son or maybe even brothers. But the second man seemed quite a bit older. There was a jar of a cloudy white liquid on the table and there were two glasses. The first man motioned for Stephen to sit and he went down a dark hall and came back with a third chair and another glass. "My name is Martin. You appear to be from the USA, may I ask your name?" Stephen answered politely, "Stephen Saldivar, glad to meet you Senor Martin. Thank you for inviting me in, and you are correct I am from the USA". Martin's expression changed and his head came forward. He looked at Stephens face very closely. Stephen was uncomfortable with him being so close and he began to back away towards the door, thanking Martin for inviting him in, but saying that he had an appointment and must be leaving. Martin laughed and the second man looked up for the first time and said in old fashioned formal Spanish, "It is still pouring rain, please stay a little longer. We will show you our library of old books and maps. You are interested in history and books are you not?" Stephen thought to himself that he needed to be careful; he remembered stories of all the kidnapping and robberies in the old neighborhoods. His Mexican acquaintances had told him not to walk alone in the areas outside the main tourist or business zones. But he glanced out through the courtyard to the outer door and could barely see across the street. The rain was pouring even harder than it had been when he came in. The four inch gutter spouts on the roofs across the way were shooting horizontal streams of water two or three feet into the air before it fell down to the street. The noise of the rain bouncing splashing up as it hit the streets and buildings was quite loud. He stood there looking outside not knowing what to do. Martin said "Don't worry Esteban; we are scholars, not bandits. I am curious because we share your family name. In fact your full name is the same as one of our great grandfathers from the 15th century. Perhaps we are cousins. Our ancestor, who also had the name Esteban, owned a very interesting manuscript that was written by his adopted son. This adopted son was perhaps the first European to see Tenochtitlan. Sit down, drink some pulque and we will show you the manuscript, and maybe we will even show you our ancient codex[5]".

Stephen looked at the two of them and decided that they were going to try and sell him something they had made and were going to pass it off as an authentic codex. He knew that there were only 6 or 7 authentic pre-conquest codices and maybe 500 made after the conquest. They were all very valuable and were kept in Museums and big libraries. If a new one actually existed it would not be in this old building, in the custody of these two old men. But he decided to stay and see what they had, maybe, just because he had never tried real Pulque and maybe because he really did not want to go out in the rain again. So he sat down. The second old

_____

[5] A codex is a "book" created on long folded sheets. They generally contained images and pictograms containing information about histories, mythologies and astronomy.

man looked at him again, drank from his glass and said "My name is Maurilio, I am nearly one hundred years old, and the pulque keeps me young, like a rabbit". This seemed to be an odd thing for him to say. Stephen knew that Pulque was an ancient Mexica alcoholic drink dedicated to the old god Centzon Totochtin (400 Rabbit). The mythology surrounding Pulque is that it can be psychedelic. When drinking it, your intoxication level is measured in "rabbits". To say that one is 400 rabbits means that a person is totally drunk. Pulque does not keep well. It is not available commercially and is generally made by the owners of the Pulquerias where old men gather to drink it. It is a Mexican tradition that has survived from before the Spanish conquest.

Martìn poured pulque for Stephen. The two of them sat down at the table with Maurilio and all three lifted their glasses. Maurilio said "Salut!" They all drank. It was white, bitter and had a thick pulpy texture. Stephen did not much care for it, but he had heard and read so much about it, he was glad to have finally tasted it.

Martìn said "Do you like it?" Stephen just shrugged and said "When do I start seeing the rabbits?" They all laughed, Martìn got up and went into the back again. Maurilio said in a loud voice aimed down the hall, "My soup is cold". A small dark woman came out of one of the rooms. She picked up Maurilio's bowl. She looked at Stephen and spoke to Maurilio

13

in a language much different from Spanish. Stephen guessed it was a native language, maybe Nahuatl, the language of the Mexica. Maurilio nodded, looked over at Stephen and answered her, mentioning his name. She looked at Stephen again and shook her head in a gesture of disapproval and then walked off with the bowl. As she walked, he noticed the sash around her waist was decorated with small shiny square cut dark stones. They immediately reminded him of what he had just seen on the dog outside. They reflected and sparkled off the walls as she walked away. For a moment he wondered where the light that reflected in the stones was coming from, but then he started thinking again that this was someplace he should not be and some kind of scam or robbery was about to happen. He started to get up to leave when Martin returned with a stack of what appeared to be very old books. He sat them down and handed Stephen one, "Look at this." he said, "The autobiography of Tomas, our ancestors adopted son. He was holy man who lived with the Mexica before Cortez came. It was found in the ruins of a Mexica palace by an Indian and given to our ancestor several years after the conquest." Stephen took the fragile looking book and touched the thick brittle cover. "I am afraid I'll tear it." he said. "Set it down and open it carefully, it's stronger than it looks", Martin answered. Maurilio nodded assent. It certainly appeared to be a handwritten manuscript. The writing was a beautiful calligraphy. Long sweeping letters, the lines themselves changed thickness as they swept across the page. Stephen could not begin to read it. However, at the end, there was a date that he recognized, it was 1536 AD. Maurilio and Martin were looking at him very closely. "Beautiful", he said. Stephen looked at it again, turned some pages. The pages were thick and coarse, perhaps made from some kind of bark paper. They were all hand stitched with a thread that may have been cactus fiber. "Tell me about the book, tell me about Esteban and his adopted son? "

Maurilio looked at him and very seriously said, "His name was Tomas, he was named for the disciple Tomas, who we know as the "doubting Tomas". The disciple Tomas traveled far to the east spreading the Gospel.

"We know you cannot read this archaic handwriting, but we have an English translation. Maurilio translated it in the late 30's", Martin said. "Iuitl (e-u-e-tl) will bring it to us." He then called down the hall in the same native language the woman had spoken. Aha, Stephen thought, this was it, they want to sell me some fanciful translation of this book. These guys are really good, what an amazing build up. He wondered what the price would be.

The woman came in with another book, it was old, and could well have been made in the 30's, it was printed rather than handwritten and it was in English.

Stephen looked at her. Speaking Spanish he said," Senora, may I ask, is Iuitl your name?" Martin answered for her, "She pretends that she does not speak or understand Spanish." Iuitl glared at him as he continued talking, "But yes that's her name, Iuitl. It means "Feather" in Nahuatl, the language of the Mexica. She floats like a feather through time. She is very beautiful is she not?" Stephen briefly thought the phrase about floating through time was odd. But he mulled it over his mind and then thought, Spanish is such an expressive language.

He looked at her closely, she appeared to be about 30, she was thin and very trim and probably less than 5 feet tall, and yes, she was very beautiful, but in a most uncommon way. He supposed it was the clarity and the rich translucent brown color of her eyes that struck him more than anything else. Her eyes were fascinating; He had never seen eyes like hers before. As she looked at him, the dark mirror like stones on her sash were reflecting light into his eyes from somewhere, maybe he thought, the bulb above them. She was looking closely at Stephen and then she nodded again and spoke at length to Maurilio, both of them talking fast and looking back and forth at each other and Stephen. Then she turned and walked back down the hall. Maurilio and Martin seemed very excited at what she said. "She says yes, now she remembers you." Stephen was really confused by this. "I can't remember ever seeing her before" he told the men. They both laughed and said that he should read the book. Martin put his hand on Stephen's shoulder and said, "She knows you from your dreams".

Stephen suddenly noticed that the din from the rain was letting up. After the comment about the dreams, he figured that these people were either a little crazy or very practiced con artists. "Thank you so much for your hospitality, but I need to go now. How much do I owe you for the book?" Martin answered, "There is no charge for the book, since you may be our cousin, we are loaning it to you. Just bring it back when you are done and we can discuss it with you. Oh, I almost forgot, would you like to see the codex?" Stephen really wanted to leave, but since the original book seemed old and authentic he decided to stay and see what they had. "Yes", I said, "let me have a quick look".

Iuitl was already walking back towards them with a large folded object. She laid it down on the table, and unfolded it. "This is her", said Maurilio, pointing to one of the figures on the first sheet of the codex. Then putting his head down and looking at the soup, he murmured, "but that was a long time ago."

Stephen looked up at Martin. He was smiling with the same satisfied expression that a doting parent might have when telling his three year old child about the rotation of the earth or something equally incomprehensible to a child's mind. "This is her?" he said, not quite understanding what that comment had meant. Martin laughed, Maurilio continued to look down at his soup and Iuitl stood away from the table glowering at all of them.

The codex contained, when unfolded, six frames. It told a story with pictures and glyphs and was meant to be read like a book. It was very beautiful and fragile looking. It was made from what appeared to be the same materials as the book but it was thinner and had a smoother surface. During the conquest thousands of these were burnt by the Spanish. The entire three thousand year history and culture of all the cities and peoples of Central America and Mexico was burnt and forgotten in just a few shorts years. The one they were looking at was certainly old. But Stephen thought that it must have been made after the conquest. The stylized figures, scale and perspective were exactly as he had seen on other images from Codices that he had seen. The pictures showed what looked like a comet streaking across each of the frames. There were explanatory glyphs running along the sides of each frame. There was a very large woman with what appeared to be snakes hanging down from where her hair should have been. She appeared to be one of the goddess's of the Mexica. He had seen images that looked like her before. Her name was Coatlicue. Standing next to this goddess, there was a small woman (this is what Maurilio had pointed to), some kind of huge four legged animal or monster and what appeared to be a European, all standing atop one of the Pyramid-like temples of the Mexica. In the background there were small figures of Mexica warriors and Spaniards on horses fighting. The last frame was interesting. It was a blue cloud with a picture of what might have been The Virgin of Guadalupe[6] floating above the temple. "This is really amazing" he said. "Do you know the story behind it? Do you know what the glyphs say?" Maurilio looked up again and said "Yes, we know everything about it. It is like an illustration of the ending of the book. Read the book, come back and we will tell you what it means. Would you like a jar of Pulque to take back to your hotel?" Stephen politely turned down the Pulque and offered again to pay for the book. He told them that he did not know when he would be back in Mexico City. They looked at each other and Maurilio said with an odd smile "Don't worry we think that after you read the book you will be back soon with many questions".

As Stephen began to turn to leave, Martin picked up a glass of Pulque and held it in front of Stephen in one hand with his own glass in the other. Both of the men looked at Stephen, gestured with their glasses. He took the glass, they

---

[6] The Virgin of Guadalupe is the Patron saint of Mexico. Legend says that the Virgin Mary appeared to a Mexican Indian in 1531 on a hilltop in Mexico City. The cloak of the Indian is said to have a miraculously painted image of the virgin. The cloak is on display at the Basilica of Guadalupe in Mexico City

toasted, as Mexicans do, with a "Salut!" and "Adios".
Stephen looked over at Iuitl, held out his glass to include her
in the toast. She appeared almost transfixed, looking
intensely at him. Stephen found it hard to break eye contact
with her. After a few seconds, that seemed to him like a few
hours, he finally looked away, set his glass down, took the
book under his arm and walked out onto the street, very
curious about the book, the codex and the people he had
just met.

When he got outside, the rain had stopped. He thought
about walking back to the hotel in the Polanco area. It was
about 2 miles and part of the walk was through Chapultepec
Park. But he thought it would be wet, muddy and getting
dark, so he decided to take a cab. He had been warned about
taking street cabs, but he decided that street cabs were
probably better than walking alone through the park at
dusk, especially when his head was spinning from the
Pulque and from his very curious encounter with Martin,
Maurilio and Iuitl. So he hailed a cab, got in and told the
driver where to go. Traffic was completely jammed and very,
very slow, maybe even slower than usual because of the wet
streets. Even with the driver darting in and out of the side
streets that Mexican cab drivers like so much, it still took
about 45 minutes to go two miles and get back to the hotel.

The desk clerks at the Hotel Nikko knew him and they agreed to extend his stay for another night. When he got back to his room it was about 6pm, too early for dinner. Usually around this time, he met friends in the bar and they sat back, relaxed, had a drink and watched the entertainment. This month it was two Russian sisters, singing Frank Sinatra songs in Spanish. But tonight he decided to get room service dinner and take a look at the book. He stood at the window in his room, looking out at the biggest city in the world from thirty four stories up. It was almost dark. All the lights of the city were on. He tried to imagine what it all looked like four hundred and seventy nine years ago in 1520. There would been have fires burning on the tops of temples all through the valley, boats with torches would have been busy paddling around the lakes, cooking fires would be burning everywhere. It would have been alive with a world and a thriving culture that was soon to end. The modern lights reflecting in the window almost danced like firelight. He glanced at the book, sat down, took off his shoes, put his feet up and began to read.

Part 2 - The Autobiography of Tomas

1492 Memories of Grenada

Translated by Maurilio Saldivar De Lara 1938

Translator's note: This is a translation of the autobiography of a truly holy man. I have tried to make the language of the 15th century as modern and understandable as I can. This account of his life was never finished. Tomas disappeared in 1522. What he tried to do was to make real a dream that would have changed the world. The peoples of Mexico and perhaps all the Americas would have been rid of the blood thirst of their old gods; free of slavery to colonists from Europe, and independent and blessed by the Holy Mother.

Herein I tell the story of my life as I remember it. I am writing this manuscript in a place I could never have dreamt of. Among a people so foreign and different I could never have imagined them.

My life has been a journey towards a fated end. That end will happen for better or worse very soon. I want my children and all my descendants to understand me and know the things I have done and why I have done them. I want them to understand the great lessons and secrets I learned about God and our saviors.

I have been many things, a moor, a student, a novice priest, and in the eyes of the false church and the inquisition, I have been a heretic. I have been a murderer, a settler, a soldier, an outlaw, and the messenger of god. I have been all these things but most importantly I have been a confidant and at times a voice for she who we in the old world call Santa Maria, the Holy Mother.

The first memories I will relate are the events that led to the beginning of my life as a Christian. It was on the second day of January 1492, the last day of the nearly eight hundred year rule of the Moors in Hispania. I was eight years old living in Grenada. I can still see my father and his two primary wives frantically loading the carts. The servants and slaves had run away to seek pardon from the Christian soldiers who were already in the city. Two of my half-sisters and three of my half-brothers were hidden at the bottom of the cart. The beds and clothing of the slaves were thrown on top to hide the richer possessions. My father had torn and dragged his fine robes through the mud so he would not appear to be a rich man. My mother, a Christian concubine and slave had been killed earlier this morning. I did not really understand death and I was still hoping she would wake up soon. My father said he had to kill her to prevent her from being raped by the Christians. The children (including myself) who were to be left behind were each given a Christian coin and told to hide in the mountains and work our way to the ocean. We were told to be careful because the Christian soldiers would roast us on an open fire, eat us and throw what was left to the dogs. The other servants and children ran off and left me. My father's wagons departed. I was alone in the huge house. I ran to where my mother's body was laying. I was terrified. I wept and then finally slept, clinging to her lifeless body.

I was awakened by trumpets, drums and singing along with the sound of many horses and wagons in the streets. My first thought was that my father had returned for me. I ran to the courtyard. There were three soldiers there and one man dressed in a brown robe. The soldiers had large red crosses on their tunics. I knew that these must be the Christians, the people who would eat me. I ran back to my mother's body for protection. Her body was cold now and I think I realized that she had gone to Allah and she would not wake up

The soldiers yelled something I could not understand, I ran, they came after me and one huge bearded man scooped me up, held me by the skin on the back of my neck and took me to the man in brown.

They talked among themselves, the man in brown, Father Esteban, who became my master, teacher and father, went to where my mother was laying. They talked again and carried me out and threw me up into a wagon filled with many of my father's possessions. It was too high, I could not jump out. I looked down and many soldiers and horses and wagons in the street. All I could do was weep for my mother and think of how a sheep looks roasting on a spit. I thought this would soon be me.

We went to the grand mosque. A place I had never been, but I knew my father went there to be with Allah. I thought to myself, perhaps my father will be here. I knew he had killed many Christians and with his long sharp sword and huge muscles, he and Allah would rescue me.

But my father was not there. Instead in the mosque there were many priests and holy brothers carrying candles swinging incense baskets and talking in odd voices and using words I could not understand.

I was carried to one of them; he looked at me closely and said with an odd accent but with words I knew, "What is your name? Are you a Christian or a Moor?" I did not know what a moor was. Not wanting to be eaten I decided to say "Yes I am a Christian; my mother was a servant to Abu Ben Mossque. She always said that I was Christian." Before I told him my name, I thought for a moment; a name is a special thing, Christian names are different from the names of my family. On the streets people call me boy. So I will say that my name is Boy. And so I told the priest that my name was boy. He laughed. The priests again spoke among themselves. Father Esteban took me by the hand and led me away.

I was taken to a house that the priests and holy brothers had decided to live in. I was given a blanket and a pallet and was told that I would be a servant and I would sleep on this pallet at night.

During the next three years, most of the priests and brothers were kind to me. They gave me the saint's name, Tomas. I learned their language and I worked hard.

At first I longed for my mother at night, but soon the memories of my father and my brothers and sisters and my old life as a Moor began to fade as memories always do. I quickly learned to understand and speak the language of the priests. The spoke two languages, one a holy language and the other a language of the common words they used among themselves. I learned both very quickly. Whenever I would learn and use a new word they congratulated me and said I was a smart boy. One of the brothers, Jose Luis, was especially kind to me. He was taller and looked stronger than the others. His face was rough and had a long scar on the left side. His laugh made the others laugh. I could tell that the other men in the house looked upon him with admiration. He would talk and tell long stories at night as we sat by the fire.

But one of the priests, Father Vincenti, still believed that I could never be a Christian and would always remain a Moor. He would call me Alkalb, which means dog in language of my father. When I came around him he would spit in my path and try to kick me. The others, especially Esteban would tell him to leave me alone. I learned quickly to stay away from him.

Father Esteban spent many hours reading the old books in the priest's house. As I grew I wanted to read the books also. I did not know what they contained, but the priests said that reading the books helped them learn about God and about the war that the great devil, Satan, waged against good people.

I worked hard for the priests, washing, sweeping, and cleaning. They taught me to read in the holy language, Latin. Some nights when they were at Prayer, I would take a book and read. One night as I was lying, sleepy, in front of the fire, the priests were talking about Satan and the Jews. I had read in one of the books that Jews ate Christian children and they were punished and purified by fire for this. While the priests were talking, I spoke up and said that the Moors had told me that Christians would eat children. There was a silence and Father Esteban said that Moors were Satan's spawn and they lied in order to separate children from God. Vincenti grumbled that he would have eaten me had he seen me first.

One day Father Esteban received a letter from the Bishop Pedro Díaz de Toledo. He was told to come to Salamanca. He said I was to accompany him as his servant. It was the first time I had ever thought of leaving Grenada. His books and his robes were loaded onto a wagon and we set off.

Of course I had been on the streets of the city many times in the past years. I had gone to the market to fetch food for the priests and I had occasionally wandered the streets deep in thought thinking about the books. But on the day when we were on the wagon leaving Grenada I noticed that the streets and the houses were much dirtier then I remembered from my time as a child before the Christians came. There was excrement and filth in the streets. The smells were sometimes very intense. But I decided that perhaps nothing had changed and I had been so young before, that I did not notice. I did not trust my memories. Now I realize I was correct the city was indeed much dirtier than before.

1496 Becoming a man

The journey to Salamanca was long. I had never imagined that the world extended so far to the north. When we arrived, Esteban was ordered to go immediately to meet the Bishop. But before he brushed the road dust and mud from his robe, he showed me the grand house we were to live in, and told me to take the books he had packed to Father Eludio in the Library.

I was still unloading and carrying books when he returned. He said that he had been given the job of assistant inquisitor and he needed to read more of the books to understand the sins of each of the accursed ones. He also told me that after I had delivered the books I was never to go into the library. He would occasionally bring me a book to read, but I would be punished severely if I were to try to read a book without his permission.

In our new home, life went on much as before. I cleaned and washed for the brothers. There were other boys there, also working. The holy men who lived there were very busy coming and going. They sat and talked and read and prayed.

Occasionally Father Esteban would bring me a book. We would discuss it. He was always happy and "astonished", as he would say, that I could understand and talk about what I had read.

One day, the other boys and I watched the Auto de Fe[7] where Jews, Moors, idolaters and witches were made to parade in the streets, bloody and beaten, wearing tall conical hats. The onlookers yelled insults and threw rocks at them. Before night and darkness came, Father Esteban told me to go into the house, he said that the vapors from burning witches could stick into the lungs of boys and that if this happened to me, Satan would be inside of me. I remember on that night seeing the smoke and hearing the screams of the witches and Jews being burned. I looked out the window, and breathed the smoke. It made me cough and scared me so much I almost immediately threw up.

When I was 16, on my eighth year of being a Christian, Esteban said that he would take me to meet the Bishop to discuss a book I had just read.

The Bishop sat in huge room with richly woven and colorful tapestries on the stone walls. There were also great colored windows that were cut and joined to show stories from the holy books. The stories were ones that I knew and could

---

[7] A ritual of public penitence that condemned heretics were subjected to, often before being burnt alive.

30

picture in my mind. But what impressed me about the windows was not the stories but the light that was nearly transparent as it flowed through the air to land on, and touch, a wall or part of some one's body, and then as it landed the color that appeared was soft and deep and warm. As I watched and let my mind play with the colors, Esteban pushed me into a deep bow and introduced me to the Bishop. This grand man, the Bishop, sat on a platform in a large chair about 3 feet above me; his robes were thick and rich with fine furs and deep color. He looked at me impatiently and said in an odd accented voice, "Tomas El Huerfano[8], I have heard good things about you. Father Esteban tells me you can read and you can understand the histories in the books he has taken to you. Tell me what the books have taught you about the infidel Moors and Turks". I started to speak, first softly with my head down, worried that I would seem stupid or childish. As I continued I became consumed with the words, they began to flow, I became more and more animated, I spoke with the gestures and rhythm, that I had learned from watching and hearing Esteban and the other priests talk. My voice, which was beginning to change from a boy's voice to deeper and richer man's voice, did not crack or change pitch when I spoke to the Bishop, as I had feared it would.

---

[8] "The Orphan"

I spoke of the fall from grace; of how the brothers Cain and Abel had fought and how Cain had killed Abel and cursed himself and all his descendants who would become the Moors and Turks; I spoke of Satan's temptations to Jesus on the mountain; how the Jews had allowed our lord and savior to be tortured and killed. I then explained that I had learned that both the Jews and the Turks, of whom the Moors belonged, now followed Satan and engaged in many devilish rituals and would not worship Jesus and God as they should.

When I was done, the Bishop sat back in his chair and did not speak for a few moments. I was afraid that I had said something wrong or that my understanding of the books was incorrect. In the silence my mind raced back to my old life in Grenada and I tried unsuccessfully once again to remember any devilish rituals in my father's house. Finally, my thoughts were broken and the Bishop looked at Esteban and then at me and said, "Yes, I believe this boy is ready to study and take his vows. Send him to the scholars and teachers. I will give him my seal and blessing."

When we left the Bishop's palace and walked out on to the streets, Esteban turned to me. "The university is a place where your mind will open to the teachings of our Lord and Savior and also to the wonders of the wide world. But it will also be a place where you will face challenges, both spiritual and physical. You are prepared for the spiritual, but you will need to learn some things about the world before you go. I have sent for Brother Luis, he will teach the things you need to know to be a man of the world. Once you understand what he teaches you and learn the skills and knowledge you need, then you can decide if a Godly life is right for you.

When Brother Luis arrived from Grenada, we went several days out of the city to a great house that was the home of Esteban's family. We stayed for three months. Luis taught me fight, to use the weapons of war and to ride. I had grown tall and during this time with Luis I grew strong. I learned to love the way my body responded and moved almost without thinking. Towards the end of my training, Luis said there were two more things I needed to learn. He took me to a tavern. He made me drink wine, too much wine. He told me wondrous things I had never imagined about women. I laughed and was happy and felt like at last I was a man who could do whatever I wanted. But towards the end of the night, I made a fool of myself. I could not walk straight, I could not think, I could not speak. I understood now why the drunks I had seen in the streets were to be pitied. I fell down and slept. I remember being carried back to a wagon and being thrown in. The next day I was very sick and thought I had poisoned myself and would soon die. Luis said we would talk about what I had learned after I felt better.

On the fifth month of my training, Father Esteban came to the house. He and Luis spoke privately for a long time. When they finished they called for me. Esteban said," Brother Luis has told me that you have done well and you are ready to go into the world and the University. Because you have no family name, it will be difficult for you. Many of the boys and scholars you meet will be proud Hidalgos[9] from old families. Because of this, I am adopting you to my family. From now on you are my son, you are Tomas Zaldivar. I am not sure how much help it will be to have my name, but it will be better than having no name."

The first year at the University in Salamanca went by in a haze. As Father Esteban had said, most of the other boys were from ancient noble families. But at times, I thought, for most of them, perhaps their studies were secondary to their lives singing, drinking, fighting and visiting the whores. Most of them knew Esteban had adopted me and my blood was not noble blood regardless of the name that I carried. So I was always an outsider, I was the one who could not recite the deeds and valor of my forebears in fighting the Moors. Many of the boys believed, like Father Vincenti had believed, that my blood was at least half Moor and that I should never be allowed to touch the holy books. They taunted me, and

[9] Hidalgos are minor Spanish nobility

once, it was in the year 1503, I was forced to fight. I was strong and I remembered my lessons from Brother Luis.

One of the boys had insulted my mother several times and said that she was a Moors whore. Usually I would walk away from him. But on this day I could no longer bear it. Swords and daggers were not allowed to the younger students so I took hold of the boy and I was choking him. His friend came to help him. He pulled me away and held me against a table. I grabbed a mug from the table and slammed it into the second boy's head. He fell to the floor holding his bleeding head. The first boy came at me again. I hit him with the mug also. By this time about 20 of the student were gathered round watching. There was a sudden pause in the excited noise and talking of those watching. I glanced up and one of the older boys had pulled a dagger from his sash and was walking towards me. A foot came out of crowd and tripped him and he fell to the floor. Two of the rectors and an armed guard came running and stopped the fight. They held me and kicked away the dagger. One of the watchers stepped forward and said, "I saw the whole thing. They insulted this man with an insult that one should die for. And then they were too cowardly to fight man to man. It was three against one. They should be hanged for dishonoring themselves." The three who insulted and attacked me were cursed by the rector, they hung their bleeding heads and left. The rector called after them and said they would be punished severely if they tried to revenge their defeat. The rector looked at me and said that if I were to be a priest I must learn to ignore those who insult me and turn my cheek as our savior had taught. With that the crowd began to walk away. The boy who had spoken up for me, walked over and congratulated me. He said that the three I fought were of a family that was an ancient enemy of his family and they were all dishonorable cowards.

My new friend was a Hidalgo, but his family was poor. He obviously did not like the boys I fought. He bowed and formally introduced himself, Hernan Cortés de Monroy y Pizarro Altamirano was his name. He said that from now on our families would be linked and would be allies. Hernan was a serious young man. He considered his speech and words carefully before speaking and was very formal in his bearing.

After this introduction he insisted that I accompany him and some of his friends to a tavern where we would celebrate our alliance and victory. I was still in throes of the hot blood I had experienced in the fight. I remember the sickness I had felt when Luis had taught me to drink wine but I didn't care. That night with Hernan and the others was the first time since I was a child that I had been away from the holy men of the church. It was a great awakening for me and I consider it the transition of my life from boy to man. But it was more than the company of Hernan and the others that made me feel this way. The tavern was not only a place for young men to drink and sing and brag about all the great things they would do in their lives. There were women and rooms upstairs. Esteban had given me money, but so far in my life I had done nothing with it except eat and live simply. That night however, drunk with wine and celebrating all that was to come in our lives, I decided to explore and experience the lessons Luis had taught me about women. Hernan and the others were thinking the same thing. When I told them I had never been with a woman, they all laughed and said it was time. I told them I had money but I did not know where to begin. Hernan went to the tavern keeper and talked to him. He pointed to me. They both looked at me, smiled and went in a back room and returned with several women. Hernan told to take my pick, the price was the same for each of them. His friends, now my friends also, continued to laugh and taunt me. The women also taunted me, they bared their breasts, showed me their tongues and writhed their bodies around. As I watched them I felt my skin grow hot. There was an inner warmth filling my groin. That part which makes me a man was swelling. My head was light and my thoughts grew confused. I wanted to grab one of them and have it done there, now on the floor. I steadied myself and tried to think clearly. I forced my brain to return to making a choice.

I considered myself a holy man, not experienced and barely conversational in the activities they were selling but I remembered Luis telling me, "When you are learning to ride, choose the calmest one first". I decided to choose the smallest and quieter of the three. She had long dark hair and a face that was not unattractive. She appeared to be a year or two older than I. She was neither thin nor fat. After all these years and all I have done I can still picture her clearly in my mind. All and all I expected her to be a good companion for my first carnal experience. When I choose her, Hernan seemed disappointed. I remember him saying, "You should have chosen Mirabella. She is my favorite. She would have taught you to ride and spur so that you would never fall off or be desaddled in the future. But I respect your decision and wish you well. Mirabella and I will take our leave now". He saluted and was gone. The others chose women and also disappeared. I was left standing there looking at the girl I had chosen. She looked at me and asked what I wanted. I told her I didn't know as I had never been with a woman before. She laughed. I asked her name. She answered "My name does not matter. You have come to me for one thing and you shall have it. Come with me now."

Since I am writing my story for my descendants I will not go into detail about this encounter.

After we were done I wanted to lay with her and talk. To tell the truth I had never actually talked to a woman except about food or cleaning. A woman was an unknown being to me. I wanted to learn more. When I told her this, she said that her master only allowed her to stay with me a short time and she must go and entertain more customers tonight so that she could earn enough to not be beaten in the morning. I told her that I would pay more – perhaps enough for the whole night. I went out and paid a sum to the tavern master. I came back to the room and lay with her. I learned much about women several times during that night. But as it became late and we tired, I asked her to tell me about her life.

Her name was Naomi. She had been born into a prosperous Jewish family, her father had been a merchant in Merida. But when the dark times came, the inquisition had taken her father and brother. Her mother and sisters were told to leave Castile and Aragon. Their house and all their belonging except two mules and a wagon were taken. They decided to go north towards Brittany and France where they had relatives.

As they neared Salamanca, they were stopped by bandits. Naomi was raped and taken away. She did not know the fate of her mother and sister. The bandits took her, used her for a few weeks and sold her to the tavern owner who had kept her as a whore now for over two years. She cried as she told me this. Memories of her family haunted her and she said that she had tried to forget and accept that she was now a whore and would never be anything more.

I tried to comfort her telling her of the forgiveness and peace our savior and lord would provide. She laughed at this and told me that the bandits, the tavern owner and the men who destroyed her family and the ones who raped and sold her were all Christians. All the men who used her and hurt her were Christians. If our Christian god was so kind and merciful why was her life like being in hell? She said she knew she could die for saying what she had said but she did not care, she said that she thought Christians were devils. I tried to comfort her and said that many men who say they are Christians did indeed act like devils, but I was not one of them. She could say whatever she thought to me. She wept again and finally fell asleep in my arms. I could not sleep. I lay there thinking and wondering about how our God and our Savior could allow his people to destroy so many lives and cause so much misery to others, all in his holy name.

I eventually fell asleep and when I awoke in the morning Naomi was gone. I got up, dressed and went out to ask for her. There were women sweeping and cleaning the tavern and when I asked them where I might find Naomi. They shook their heads and continued their work.

I learned two very important things from my night with Naomi. First of all, I think I then knew why holy men must remain chaste. Our faith, our meditations and our prayers can only bring us a glimpse of the ecstasy that is heaven, while being with a woman can for a very short moment actually put us into a state of ecstasy. The second thing I realized was that evil existed in all men, even Christians. It was after this encounter that I first began to think that perhaps being a holy man was not really what I wanted. But I returned to the university and the lectures and buried myself in study and kept my mind focused on learning all I could.

Over the next few years at the University I must admit that I went back to the tavern many times and lay with the women there. Each time I went I asked about Naomi and was answered with silence and shrugs. I think of her often and hope she was able to escape the evil that held her.

Hernan Cortez became a good friend. We drank together and laughed together. His life however was focused on adventure and romance and not books.

I will long remember the last time I saw Hernan in Castile. One evening he came to my room. He said he had to visit a friend. His smile and the sparkle in his eyes informed me that his friend was a woman. He said he hoped I would repay the help he had given me by keeping watch outside the ladies house. He said I was to signal him if "her father" came home. I told him that this was not a job for a novice priest. He should find another friend to help him. But he insisted and reminded me of the kindness he had done for me and the alliance of our families. I finally and reluctantly agreed to help him. After darkness came that evening we walked into the city. We stood outside a house and he told me to wait in some nearby trees. If anyone came to the door, I was to howl loudly like a wolf. He thanked me again and went to the door where he was soon admitted. I stood there for nearly two hours until a horseman rode up. He appeared to be a Hidalgo and perhaps a captain. He went in the door. I began to howl. After a short time I heard yelling and I saw my friend Hernan leap from the second story window. His landing injured his leg. The "father" who I later learned was the ladies husband stood at the window shouting obscenities such as I had never heard. I helped Hernan. We ran into the trees. He told me to help him to a tavern that was close by. We walked to the tavern, always looking behind to make sure we were not followed or being chased. We went inside. The tavern master was a friend to Hernan. After Hernan briefly explained to his friend what had happened, he turned to me to thank me and told me that now the obligation was reversed and he was in my debt. He warned me not to talk about what had happened and said that I should go. I did not see Hernan again for several years, at which time he indeed returned the favor. Later we would become enemies, but at that time and place we were truly comrades in adventure.

Without Hernan in my life, I felt a little empty. The fun and adventures of our time together were gone. But during the next year I found books that were not histories or holy books. They were books about adventure and romance. They were books that put thoughts into my mind that the holy brothers and scholars would not have approved. *La Celestina* and *Amadis of Gaula* were two such books. These stories and my remembrances of the laugher I had shared with Hernan intensified my doubts about becoming a holy man. I was torn between these ideas of adventure on the one hand and on the other hand the love of reading and knowledge of the world that I was experiencing at the university.

The scholars and holy brothers who accepted me (some of course did not), conducted serious and informative lectures and gave me fascinating books. Some of these were histories of the world. Many times they seemed as exciting as the adventure book. The histories of the Church also fascinated me. When I combined my thoughts about the world history and the history of the church, I had many questions that the books did not answer and the scholars who lectured warned me not to ask.

There were other books that explained the devils rituals and the magic and illusion used to perform them. It was then that I began to believe that perhaps many of the deeds that we believe are performed by devils are merely tricks that are learned to astonish and take power over others. I studied these tricks so that I would be able to face those accused of witchcraft and understand that sometimes real evil is man-made rather than the work of Satan. I mentioned this idea to one of my teachers, he scolded me and said that all evil comes from Satan and if men perform illusions then Satan is controlling them and teaching them. He warned me to be careful about talking to others when I had ideas like this.

Some the things I read, told about rituals in which the Jews secretly kidnapped children and ate them. I remembered what I had erroneously thought and been told about Christians eating children and then by the Christians about Moors eating children. I wondered at the truth of any of this. But I was determined that given time, my faith would outweigh the doubts.

Then a Holy event occurred that ended my doubts and gave my life a goal. It was a goal that took several years for me to understand. But I knew that God had entrusted me with an important task that someday would be made clear.

1505 The first visitation

On the night of St Bonaventure in the year 1505, the dormitories were nearly empty. I was lying awake on my pallet. The full moon was shining with its yellow light through the long, narrow window. I remembered the glass at the bishops house and how the light transformed the room. Suddenly the moon disappeared. I thought perhaps a cloud had covered it, I got up and stretched to look. Suddenly a bluish glow appeared behind me. I could smell roses. I turned and there, floating in front of me, in an incandescing blue light that I could never describe with mere words was the Holy Mother, smiling at me in a way that made my body warm and happy. I fell to my knees. She spoke.

"You have learned many things, my son. Some of what you have learned you question. This is your destiny. You must always question those that wish to divide my children. You must remember that all men are children of God and that our lord, my son Jesus wishes all men to be saved in the ways that they can understand. Devotion to our lord God has many correct forms. The evil one wants men to be separated. He wants Christians to believe that all others are evil as he wants the Turks and Jews and others to believe that Christians are evil. Evil exists as greed, hatred and hurtful deeds, not as a belief in stories and books. Be careful in your words and beliefs, there are those who say they are with God, but who have hatred and greed in their hearts. You have a great and important task to perform. Continue to read and think and watch. Tell no one of my visit. I will always be with you."

And then as fast as she had appeared, she was gone, the moon reappeared and my mind was full of thoughts and questions, especially about the great task she spoke of.

1506 The Inquisitor's assistant

As the next two years went by I proved to the scholars that I had an outstanding ability to remember what I had read and also more importantly to understand and connect the ideas in the books. I know that some were concerned about questions I had asked, but they thought that once I had been warned I never asked again. Most of them felt that their teachings and my faith would drive the questions from my mind. Others were not so forgiving.

Especially troubling to some of them were questions about the words of the Holy Mother. Without mentioning the great gift I had been given by her appearance, I would try to ask the scholars and father professors about her words. There were times when I was berated and scolded but there were also times when some of the fathers would look at me deeply and say that the inquisition and the church would not take kindly to such thoughts. They would say that perhaps I should go out into the world and become a hermit monk to pray and mediate on these ideas.

In the year 1506 I was appointed as apprentice to the Inquisitors of Grenada. I was to be one of the youngest of their apprentices. I was expected in Grenada in ten days so I needed to leave immediately. But I also felt that I must say good bye to my father, Esteban. I had not seen him much in the last few years, but I knew that he was now a respected man, who one day was expected to be a Bishop. I felt that I owed him everything I had become; I even owed my life to him. I walked up the hill to the library and asked for him. I was led up the stairs to his office. He did not seem surprised by my visit, but jumped up and said, "I was hoping you would come to say goodbye." We embraced. "Before you go I have something for you. Here on the table is a ring with my seal. Keep it with you and if you are ever in need of help, send it to me". We parted then like a father and his son. I regret that I have never seen Esteban again

After the journey through the plains of Castile and the mountains of Andalusia, I rode into Grenada. I expected it to be a homecoming. The conquest had been over now for several years. I expected to see the streets and markets back to normal and filled with friendly busy people. I looked forward to seeing the flowers and grand houses I remembered. But riding through the city was not what I expected. There was filth everywhere. People were sullen and would not look at me. Soldiers and whores staggered down the street into doorways and taverns.

When I arrived at the quarters I had been assigned I unpacked my bag and spoke to some of the brothers there. My teacher and old friend, Brother Luis was one of them. As we sat and talked, I learned that Father Vincenti was the senior assistant to the Inquisitor, The Bishop Antonio De Rojas.

The next day, I went to Vincenti's chambers. It was a dark place, near the palace of Boabdil the moor and the last Emir of Grenada. I was told to sit in the doorway and wait until I was summoned. I waited half the day, and when the sun was nearly to the mountain tops in the west. I was told that the father would see me.

Vincenti laughed when I came in to his office. He said, "So It's you, the dog boy, the Moor, perhaps I will have the opportunity to eat you yet. You have grown. I have letters telling me of your learning and your great faith. But to me these mean nothing. I know who you are. I know your father was a Moor Devil and a slayer of hundreds of good Christians. But I am ordered to keep you here as an assistant apprentice. So here is your assignment and duty, your holy calling if you want to call it that. You will work in the sewer of the devils; you are to go through the shit of the Jews and Moors to tell us if they are truly conversos. You will look at all they have thrown and excreted into the sewers and examine it all for signs of devil worship, black magic, and the bones of children. The evidence you gather will help us cleanse ourselves from these animals of Satan."

The next few months were the worse time of my life, but as a novice and apprentice I was determined to maintain my vows of obedience. I brought Vincenti bones and parchment and paper with Hebrew writings. He was never satisfied or really convinced that I was an honest Christian. He tried to trick me into making statement or saying things that would allow him to convince others that I was really a Moor.

One day, I was called by Vincenti to attend and speak at the trial of a Jew. He was an old man. His name was Abram. He claimed to be a Converso, but he had been arrested in a cellar praying with other Jews. When the soldiers burst in, it was said that he had thrown fire at them and tried to run away. He was caught and beaten, in fact nearly killed, and now he was here facing the priests of the Inquisition. It was certain that tomorrow he would be tied to a stake and burned. I was to tell the priests that there were never pork bones in the sewers running from his home. During the trial he was asked how the devil gave him fire to throw, He told the questioner that it was a trick. He said he knew many tricks like this. He said that it had nothing to do with the devil. He asked for a flint and said he would demonstrate. One of the assistant inquisitors whipped him and told him to admit the truth. I spoke up and said that I had studied these trick at the university. I said that I thought he was probably telling the truth. There was silence. Frey Vincenti looked very angry and told me to leave.

Later that evening I could hear the screams and smell the flesh of the old man and his friends burning.

In the third month of my service, I noticed a difference in Vincenti's attitude towards me. He actually said that I was doing a valuable service and several so-called conversos had been discovered who were refusing to eat pork and still engaging in their devil rituals. I was not sure if Vincenti had actually been convinced of my honesty and faith or if there was something I was missing in his behavior. I prayed for understanding and for the grace to forgive him. But I was soon to see that my mistrust was well founded. One evening he invited me to his rooms to eat with him.

As I walked in, Vincenti greeted me quite effusively, "......Now sit with me here at the table. Tell me about your studies in Salamanca. We will eat together. I have the leg of a pig that has just been butchered and cooked especially for us."

He then rang a bell and his servants brought in a platter with meat sliced from a leg bone. I realized this was a test, if I appeared not to enjoy it, it would be one more piece of evidence for Vincenti to bring to the Bishop. The servant placed a large slice on my plate and another on Vincenti's plate. I noticed Vincenti nod and one of the servants immediately moved to stand behind me. I was not comfortable being looked down upon from behind, but there was nothing I could do. "It looks delicious Father, thank you, would you like me to grace this meat?" "Yes" replied Vincenti, "you may pray". I blessed the meal and the company and our King. We began to eat. There was an odd flavor to the meat, a bitterness I had not tasted before, but I tried to eat with relish and enjoyment. Vincenti also ate but he seemed to be paying more attention to each bite I took then to his own meal. After a few minutes, I began to feel somewhat nauseous. It struck me that Vincenti had poisoned the meat and that if I vomited it would be all the proof he needed to bring me to the inquisitors. I fell to the stone floor and indeed I vomited. All the meat came back; the odor was truly that of hell. I was dizzy, losing focus and strength. I heard Vincenti laugh and then yell for his guards. I remember being lifted up and then all was dark.

1506 Outlaw

When I awoke I was laying naked in a small room on another much rougher stone floor. I was wet from the water that had been thrown on me. I had never been so cold and I had never felt so hopeless and alone. I lay shivering and cold for many hours. My body ached with the cold yet my mind was full of thoughts of what the heat would feel like as my flesh burned in an Auto de Fe. I had only this numbing painful cold in my flesh and terrifying burning in my mind, thinking of the fire I might face. I controlled the terror by picturing the Holy Mother in my room and straining to remember the inflection of her voice and carefully visualizing each word she spoke. Finally I must have finally fallen asleep. In a half dream state I had counted the faint echo of the three chants that measured time. Then the door was flung open. Vincenti appeared with four guards. "I now know what I have always suspected; you are a Saracen moor and a false Christian. You have lied in your vows. You will appear before the Bishop and the Council of Inquisition tomorrow." To the guards he said "Wash him and give the hair robe".

After he left, the guards came and threw another bucket of water on me. The robe I was given felt as if it was lined with thorns. It did not warm me. But soon I slept again.

I woke being pulled up, my arms were tied behind me and I was dragged out of the room and up what seemed like a hundred stone steps. My feet which were bare began to sting and I could see that they were bleeding. Soon I was brought to large room with several priests sitting in a semi-circle around me. Vincenti began to tell about where I had been found, about my father, about rumored stories of the appearance of the holy mother, which of course he said was nothing but lies to defile the image of her holiness. Then he talked about what he called my inability to eat pork, about the unholy smell of Sulphur and brimstone that had accompanied my vomit. His servant came in and told the same story of the pork. The bishop looked at me and asked if I had anything to say. I tried to speak and realized my tongue was swollen from whatever poison I had been given. My attempt at speaking was completely incomprehensible. One of the priests spoke to me in the Moorish language of my childhood, asking if I needed water. I could not answer but instinctually I nodded yes, yes. Vincenti instantly stood up, "You see my brothers, the language of the moors inspires him. He is indeed a follower of the great demon and the false prophet of the Moors and Turks." One of the priests stood up and walked over to me; he held my head up and pulled open my mouth. He then dropped me and said to the Bishop, "Your holiness, I believe that brother Tomas has been poisoned. Once he has recovered we can question him and hear testimony. He has been recommended to us by Father

Esteban Zaldivar and many other learned fathers and brothers from Salamanca. We must give him a chance to speak in his defense." Vincenti began to stand up and started to shout. The Bishop raised his hand to make all of them silent. He then said that he agreed with Father Olivo. He said I was to be taken to a comfortable place and cared for and he would send a letter to Salamanca. He then looked ominously at Vincenti and said, "Tomorrow you will appear before me and explain the poisoning of this man."

It was almost one week before I recovered my strength and my tongue was normal again. During this time I asked for books but I received nothing. On the 8th day I asked to go walk in the streets. The guards said it was forbidden. But later that day a new set of guards came followed by Brother Jose Luis. He told the guards that he was authorized to take me out to our chapel to pray for my soul. He gave the guards a few coins and we left. The lodging of the brothers, the place where I had first arrived in Grenada just a few months earlier full of hopes, was very close. We talked along the way and I told Brother Luis what had happened. He said he had heard the story. He said that Vincenti had denied poisoning me and he had sworn on the name of our savior that he was telling the truth. The Bishop Rojas was forced to believe him. He then said that letters from Bishop Talavera and Father Esteban had arrived yesterday. It said that Esteban was coming to Grenada and would arrive in three days.

This news filled me with hope. I had spent many hours thinking of the Auto De' Fey I had seen in Salamanca. The smell of the smoke of the burning Jews and witches seemed to return and linger in my nostrils.

We arrived at the home; I went inside and found that my few belongings were gone. Brother Luis shook his head and said that Vincenti's servants had taken it all except, he said, for a ring, that he then handed me. It was Father Estebans ring. Luis had taken it and hidden it when he heard what had happened to me.

He said we should go to the cathedral to pray. We left the house and walked to the cathedral. When we arrived I recognized one of my guards standing in front of the door. He recognized me also and demanded to know what I was doing. Luis jumped in front of me. "He is in my custody, we have come to pray, stand aside". The guard shoved Luis aside and down the stair. He looked at me and said "Father Vincenti has told us we are to kill you if you try to escape and I believe you are escaping now". With that he drew his sword and came at me. I managed to side step and as he lunged I threw him off balance and pushed him. He fell down the stone steps. He had no helmet and fell with the side of his head hitting the stone. Luis was getting up. The guard lay there with blood streaming from his mouth and I could see several other armed men rushing towards me. The horse of someone who must have been in the cathedral was close by. I jumped on it and rode out of the city as fast as I could. I heard people yelling as I rode away. I knew that very soon armed men would be following me.

As I rode by an olive grove outside the city, I stopped and got off the horse. I pulled up a small thorn bush from the side of the road and stuck it under the horses saddle then slapped it down – the horse raced off and I hoped the trail of dust that followed it would lead the pursuers away from me. I turned and ran into the grove.

The grove was very old. The trees had thick twisted and knurled trunks. After running a great distance over two small hills, I felt that I would be invisible to anyone following me. I stopped to rest and soon fell asleep under one of the olive trees.

I was awakened by a farmer. He held an oak stave in his hand and asked what I was doing in his orchard. I told him I was lost and had stopped to rest. I am sure he did not believe me. He motioned for me to stand and pointed back the way I had come, back to the road. I decided to speak first, "Are you a Christian?" I asked him. He appeared frightened at this question. He answered in a very small voice with his head facing down "No, I am not. But the priest is teaching me and he allows me to stay here until I understand and can be baptized". "Well", I said, 'Are you Jew or Moor ?". " I follow the teachings of the Book and I am learning about our savior. But in the past I was a Jew. And you, if I may ask, who might you be? ". I thought about how to gain his sympathy and help. "I am a converso, like you are soon to be. But there are those in Grenada who do not believe me. So I have left. I am going to Seville or Salamanca where I have friends and will be safe. Can you help me, my brother? I need food and perhaps different clothes."

He began to walk, "Come with me", he said. We walked through the trees and small hills to his home on top of one of the hills. There were chickens but I did not notice a pig. We got to the door and called out to his wife. They spoke in the Hebrew tongue. I knew a few words but the accent and the pace of the words was more than I could comprehend.

"Sit here; she will bring you water, bread, cheese and olives". His wife appeared at the door. Before he could speak to her, the olive farmer made a mournful sound and pointed towards the hills from where we had come. There was dust in the air behind the hills. "It's a rider, probably looking for you. From the dust it looks like just one man. Go to the back of the house and hide behind the firewood, if he wants to look for you by walking around the house, you should go in the back door and come back here to the front. If he looks for you in the house then you walk around the house and back to the front. I will be talking to him so you can know where he is."

I didn't know if I could trust the farmer but I had no choice – so I ran to the back and crouched down behind his fire wood. I could see the back door was open. I could hear him talking to his wife and I could tell that she was not happy and that she was afraid.

Soon I could hear the horse's breathing and the rider yelling to the farmer to stay where he was. The horseman arrived at the house. He called the farmer a Jew dog and said that if he was hiding a murderer, he would watch his entire family die a horrible painful death. The farmer said he had seen no one, but there had been dust on the road earlier. The rider, who talked like an uneducated soldier, said that he would search the house and sheds but now he was thirsty and hungry. He ordered the farmer to bring wine and food. I could hear the farmer begin to walk away towards the house. The soldier said, "No not you! Your wife will serve me. I'll go into the house; it's too hot here in the sun". The farmer replied "But there is shade over there my lord, under the trees". "I will eat and drink in your house – try to stop me if you don't like it." After a pause he said "You stay here, take my horse to the shade and guard him, if you leave my horse alone you will be very sorry". I could hear footsteps and then I heard the door close.

He was in the house only a short time when I heard the wife scream. The door opened again and the farmer and the soldier were yelling, suddenly there was a dull thud and the wife began to scream again. I was tempted to run back to the front and take the soldiers horse and ride away, but instead I grabbed the axe leaning on the wall next to my hiding place. I rushed in the back door and saw the soldier forcing the woman down to the floor. He looked up at me yelled something, started to get up and reach for his sword. I was on him before he was up, I swung the dull end of the axe into his head and he fell back onto the woman. I pulled him off her. She jumped up and went to her husband, lying bleeding at the front door. I stood over the soldier in case he was stunned, but he was bleeding profusely and twitching. I knew he would soon be dead.

The farmer began to moan. The woman held his head in her lap and asked me to get water. It looked as if the soldier had hit him on the side of his head with the broad face of the sword. I got water from a jug and brought it to the woman. She cleaned his wound with the water and her dress. He opened his eyes and looked at the dead soldier, his wife and then at me. He asked if I had done it and I answered. He tried to stand but his wife held him down. He pushed aside her hand and sat up. "We must do something very soon; they will come looking for him".

As his wife tied a cloth around his wound, he thought for a moment and then said, "We should take him back to the road. Ruth will stay here and clean the blood. When we get the body to the road, I will walk towards town. When they find me I will tell them that you tried to rob me and hit me with a flat rock and then, when the soldier came, you hid behind a tree. The soldier found me laying in the road bleeding. He stopped to help me and you struck him from behind with my axe and then cut his throat. You then took his clothes and horse and rode away towards Valencia."

I agreed with his plan, even though I worried that he would not be believed. When I told him this he said, "Don't worry the Bishop likes our olives.

We dragged the soldier out and managed to throw him across the saddle of his horse. When we got to the road, we threw him down and took his clothes. The farmer took his sword and cut the dead soldiers throat to make sure that there was blood around the body.

He handed the sword to me and said, "You saved our lives, I hope I can help you. Ride fast until you reach the crossroad, then go east towards Valencia. Ride until you come to the river, go into the water there and double back to the road to Salamanca. I cannot help more than that. God be with you". I wished him good blessings also and rode away. I have never found out what happened to the farmer and his wife. I pray for them every day.

The farmer's instructions seemed logical, however I decided that perhaps it was not wise to actually go Salamanca. I was known there and the news of my crimes would reach there before I could. I decided that my destination should actually be Valencia and from there onto a ship to Napoli.

I took care to ride by night. I slept in the trees and fields away from the road. There was water, but hunger became my enemy. I had the sword, but no weapons to hunt. I had no coins to buy food from the farms and villages.

On the fourth night, there was a full moon and as I was riding along a road I met an old woman who had been carrying loaves of bread. She was sitting along the road trying to repair her sandal in the dark with only a dim lantern and moon light to see by. I stopped to see if I could help her. I must have appeared to her to be a road bandit, she seemed frightened. She could see that I was hungry. She offered me bread and said that her sons, who were big strong men, were just over the hill and would soon be there. Looking down at her sandal in the lantern and moon light, I saw what appeared to be blood from cuts on her foot. I got off the horse and drew the sword – she began to scream. But as soon as she saw that I was cutting a piece of leather from the reins of my saddle, she stopped and I could hear her pray. I held my hand out and handed her the leather. "You can lash this to what remains of your sandal. It should protect your foot until your sons arrive. If they are truly big and strong they will carry you home". She thanked God and praised me for being such a kind and generous stranger. She offered me bread again and said that if I were to let her ride my horse to her home she would give me cheese and wine and meat.   I laughed and lifted her up onto the horse, asked the way to her home, and leading the horse, I walked in the direction she pointed.

We had not gone far when I began to hear voices and see the flashes of torches. I was not sure if I should hide or continue walking. "It is my sons and my husband coming to find me." The woman said. She swung her lantern side to side to signal them. They galloped to us. As they reached us the three sons and husband all spoke at once, thanking God and saints that they had found her and at the same time reprimanding her for being alone on the road after dark. She explained about her sandal and the cuts on her foot, she showed them the bread and told them all to thank me; the stranger who had rescued her and put her on his horse. They looked down at me. The husband, Don Diego Davila de

Velazquez was his name, introduced himself and his sons. He thanked me and pledged his and his family's friendship and support. I bowed to him, and told them that I was proud to have assisted such a noble and important family as they seemed to be. He then asked my name. I did not know what to say. They may have already heard of me as a criminal and heretic at large on the road. I bowed again and the safest name I could think of was Esteban Zaldivar de Gomez, the name of my adopted father. He laughed and came down from his horse. He bowed slightly to me and said that he had known by my bearing and speech that I was Hidalgo. He told me of an ancestor who had fought the Moors in Aragon beside a Zaldivar many, many years ago and that now our families were linked as allies and friends. He begged me to honor them and come to their home for food and rest. I thanked him and, trying to play the part, I said that I too had heard the stories of our family's friendship in the past. I found it odd that the sons had not spoken, but I remembered how haughty and dignified the young hidalgos had acted at the university. I could see them talking among themselves but soon they came closer and one each dismounted and introduced himself.

"Pedro, you will walk home, help your mother on to your horse" Don Diego ordered one of his sons.

Once the lady was on the horse, Don Diego asked me to follow them. We all remounted and rode a short distance to their home.

It was a large stone manor house. Perhaps many, many years ago it had been a grand house for a noble family, but now it seemed to be coming to ruin. Stone had come loose from the walls. The holes left by the fallen stones had been patched poorly. There was thatching on the roof where tiles had once been.

We all dismounted and a servant took the reins and led the horses, including mine, into the stable next to the house.

We went into the house. Another servant had candles and lamps lit for us and I could smell the lamb estofado cooking.

It was here that I got a clear look at the family. The two sons in the house were certainly as their mother had told me, big strong men, perhaps a little older than I. Their names were Alonso and Fernando. I imagined that the brother who was walking back had most likely been the youngest. Don Diego was also a striking man; his back was still straight and his beard well-trimmed. He had a scar on his forehead just above his right eye. He was indeed an old Hidalgo soldier.

"There is water in the back if you want to clear the dust from the road, then, when you are ready, come to our table and eat".

I went to the back of the house and the servant showed me a bucket of water. I rubbed the water on my face and hands, dried them as best I could and returned to find the family sitting around a scarred but grand table. The Estofado was on the table as was bread and wine. I had not eaten in almost three days but I realized that I needed to maintain the dignity that the name I had chosen implied. So I sat and did by best to wait. Donna Maria, the mother and wife, asked her eldest son to grace the food. When he had completed the family blessing and mentioned a special blessing for me, we all began to eat and talk. Donna Maria asked if I had been given any religious instruction and training. The way I wore my hair may have caused her to wonder. I replied that yes, at Salamanca I had studied for the priesthood, but I had decided not to take my vows until I learned to know the world and its ways. I told them that I wanted to understand the lives of those I would help. They all nodded their agreement saying that I was wise, too many of the holy men they had met did not really know about the lives of real people, they were too absorbed in an ideal world that excluded the pleasures and temptations of the real world. And some of the other holy men, well, they try to hide the fact that they know the world all too well.

It was a full and wonderful night. The conversation was stimulating and absorbing. We discussed the King and lamented the death of our holy Queen Isabella. We carefully spoke of the Inquisition and the fear it brought to everyone. I learned that two of the three sons were soon to go to the Indies to make a fortune and then return to restore the family's wealth. The time passed quickly and it became very late before we knew it. Donna Maria began to yawn. We all knew it was time to take our rest. I was given blankets and shown to a room that had obviously not been used in many years, but it was shelter from the night and I was very tired.

At some time during the night, I was awakened by the eldest son Alonso shaking me. "Wake up" he said. "We know who you are; we have read the anuncios in the village. Your presence here threatens our family. You must either leave now or come with us on our journey to Cadiz and then to Hispaniola. You will be safe traveling with us, but we must leave quickly so that no one will see you here at our home!"

I was to act as one of the brothers. Pedro would be my name. We decided to go east to Valencia and find a fisherman or some coastal boat that would take us to Cadiz where we would depart for one of the colonies in the Indies. Hopefully it would be Hispaniola or maybe Isle de Juana or Isle de Santiago[10]. We were questioned only once on the road to Valencia. But the Davila name and family was well known and we were passed on without incident.

Valencia was a busy port. I was a bit concerned about being recognized. Visitors to the Holy Father in Rome departed from Valencia. Some of these were men who may have known me from Salamanca. When we saw the parties of holy men we stayed clear of them. In the harbor there were barges, galleys and other vessels bound for Rome or Napoli. The fishing boats were in a separate part of the harbor. They were mostly small, too small for the three of us and our baggage and horses. But there was one large trading ship. Alonso, the eldest of the Davila brothers made arrangements for our passage to Cadiz. This was to be my first voyage on the sea. After we boarded and were underway the vessel stayed in sight of the shore. The trip was mild and refreshing. I decided that I liked sailing and perhaps I would become a sailor. I soon learned however that sailing along the shore of our eastern sea was much different then sailing on the great limitless oceansea to the Indies.

We arrived in Cadiz on a Sunday in August 1507. As we sailed into the port I could see perhaps 10 ships loading

---

[10] Isle de Juana is now known as Cuba and Santiago is called Jamaica

men, horses and supplies. Before we landed, the Captain of our ship told me that it was late in the sailing season the favorable winds would be moving south soon. The dock and quays were packed with men trying to get their passage so they could go to the Indies for adventure and of course to make a fortune. The cathedral and church bells were singing throughout the city. Many of the men and horses wore the cross of Santiago but I only saw a few black robed holy men waiting to board the ships. I wondered what was foremost in the minds of these adventurers, wealth or salvation.

The owner of one the ships being loaded, **Dios Del Vento**, was a cousin of Don Diego Davila. He knew the brothers were coming and our passage on his ship was secured.

When we arrived on the quay, we pushed our way through the crowds. A thief tried to pull some baggage from one of our horses. Fernando saw him and grabbed the thief's arm. There was no room to draw a sword. He yelled that he had a thief. The men around us took turns punching and tearing at his clothing. Fernando moved aside, brushed himself off and we walked away. We were to meet their cousin at an Inn near the docks. When we arrived at the Inn we were told that it was full. There were no corners to sleep in and the wine had been watered down to a thin liquid of nearly no color. Alonso asked about his cousin, Don Miguel Davila. The proprietor told us to wait outside; he would try to find suitable refreshment for us. He said Don Miguel usually came at sundown.

The street where we waited was not as congested and busy as the docks, but there seemed to be an unending line of wagons and horses and men moving through the street towards the sea. The sun was nearly over the mountains to the east when Don Miguel arrived. He shook the hands of Alonso and Fernando and looked at me and asked where Pedro was. Fernando spoke and said that Pedro had decided to stay home and care for and protect their parents. He said that I was a friend. I bowed and told him my assumed name, Esteban Zaldivar de Gomez. He bowed in return and said I was welcome. Alonso made it clear to the captain that I would use Pedro's license to travel to the Indies. He shrugged and then laughing he looked at Alonso and said that his cousin Don Diego was still fully capable of protecting his wife and land. We all nodded and said yes that was surely true but there was work that a young strong man like Pedro could do so that Don Diego could relax and drink his wine.

He told us that the **Dios de Vento** would be departing in three days. He said we could sleep on the ship before we left if we wanted but he thought that we probably would regret doing so once the voyage was underway. He said there was an Inn two leagues away in the mountains towards Jerez where we could find sleep and food. Also, and he winked at us, and said that the women of Andalusia were plumb and agreeable. He told us that we would not see many women except the Indios once we arrived at our destination. He said that the women of the Indies were willing but their teeth were sharp and we must be very careful not to be bitten. The brothers laughed. My experience with women, as I have said, was limited and I wondered what he meant by this.

The Inn was an agreeable place and during our stay I had some time to sit and think. We laughed and drank and had encounters with the Andalusian women. Their teeth were not sharp but my imagination allowed me to begin to understand what Don Miguel had meant.

1507 In the islands of the New World

To tell the truth, I do not remember much of the voyage to the Indies. I was sick much of the time. When I was not sick I was thirsty or I was burning with the sun's heat or freezing and wet from the cold rain or nauseous from the smell of the men, woman and horses packed into the vessel. It was a most unpleasant experience.

But I very clearly remember the day that the ship's look out cried out that he had finally seen land, it was the island called San Salvador. There was a small harbor and a few buildings and houses on the island. For good mariners and navigators it was always the first stop. It was a place to replenish water and to allow the horses, dogs and passengers a chance to walk on solid ground again. My first impression was the scent. It was sweet and reminded me of my childhood, when Grenada was filled with flowers and sweet citrus blossoms. It was not exactly the same as I remembered, the scents were different yet the sensation was the same. I thought to myself, this must be what heaven smells like. However I was soon to see that heaven for some could well be hell for others.

When we left the ship and walked at last on the land of the New World, I saw Indians for the first time. At the university had been much discussion about whether or not the Indians, these new creatures, were actual people or some sort of animal or sub human. Those scholars who had seen the actual "Indians" said that they were indeed human and that our calling as Christians was to save and convert them from whatever devilish, idolatrous beliefs and ideas they had. Then there were others who had only seen fanciful drawings of the natives. These men, with no real knowledge to base their words on felt that the natives were animals or sub humans and only good as slaves.

I soon learned that for the settlers, reality was a mixture of both these ideas. As far as I could tell, the natives were indeed as human as I. The priests who had come to the island attempted in awkward ways to convert them without really understanding their language or culture. Many of these holy men had no patience. Instead of trying to see the Indians as children who needed to be taught, they saw their beliefs as devil worship. They destroyed their sacred places. The Indians who resisted were killed or mutilated. They were captured from their villages and taken from their homes, and treated as slaves. Their condition was misery. There was no Christian brotherly love; there was only subjugation and oppression for them. I thought of Naomi and asked myself again; why these Indians would believe that our God should be accepted when the people who profess faith and salvation and tell them that our god is merciful, end up treating them like dogs.

Our plan was to stay one day, one night and leave on the tide the next day. There was cargo to unload and a few of the passengers would be staying here. Many of the men, including the Davila brothers and I, went to a makeshift Inn to try the local wine. It was made from sugar cane, and known as Matar al Diablo. It was strong and I believed it could indeed kill a devil as its name implied.

In a voyage such as we had nearly completed you become acquainted with everyone on the ship. One of the men was Pedro de Alvarado y Contreras. He was a large strong man who took offense easily. He was someone I would try to avoid when I could. He was easy to spot because of his light red or blonde hair and beard. He talked non-stop without the bother of conversation. His tales were about himself and his exploits in the arts of war and fighting. He was too young to have actually fought in the conquest of the Moors, but he had many stories of fighting the rebellious Moors on his father's encomienda[11] in Extremadura. His stories late at night in the dark holds of the ship were mostly about the

---

[11] An Encomienda was a labor system in Spain and later in the Americas. It consisted of the King or his representative giving conquered people to soldiers and others. They became laborers and virtual slaves for those who had helped conquer them.

women he had taken and on occasion raped. His three brothers were also on the ship. I suppose that they must have heard his tales many times before, they were not among the group that listened and applauded his bravery and envied his carnal exploits.

As we sat and drank the liquor, Pedro said that he needed a woman and would leave us to find a suitable Indian. Before he walked out Alonso told him he should speak to one of the local encomiendors before acting. Pedro laughed and went out. We all shrugged and looked at each other with unexpressed and hidden emotion. Some of us may have been jealous of his boldness and others including myself wondering what exactly were we to make of our relationships to the Indians.

After a while the sun moved to set in the west across the sea. We were very happy to be walking on land again and were reluctant to go back on the stinking ship to sleep. We were all somewhat drunk. The tavern master said that the nights were warm and we could sleep on the beach sand as long we stayed above the tidal lines. We agreed and bought another gourd of the Matar al Diablo and walked down the hill towards the beach away from where the boats from the ships landed.

As we sat down on the beach to watch the sunset, we heard a commotion back at the village. We could hear many voices yelling, some were Indian and some Castilian and we could hear Pedro quite clearly. Alonso and Pedro's brother Juan got up and began to walk back the tavern. As we watched them we could see three men coming towards us. It was Captain Davila and Pedro and one of Pedro's brothers. Captain Davila told us that we needed to gather our weapons and return to the settlement immediately. There was trouble with the Indians. Pedro had taken one of their women against her will. She was the daughter of one of the leaders.

I had not come to the Indies to wage war on the inhabitants. At this point the only feeling I had for them was pity. But the next day was a blur of blood and death. The Indians had no defense against the swords, horses and dogs. It was not war it was a slaughter. Afterwards we helped burn the bodies. The smell brought back memories of the open windows in Salamanca and the burning of the witches. I realized that the smell of burning bodies was the same no matter what sort of person was on the pyre. We returned to the ship to continue on to Hispaniola

We landed in Santo Domingo two days later. It was a dirty and ill kept place. There were wood frame building in various stages of construction, but mostly there were thatched huts, made in the style of the Indians and arranged around a cleared area. Three other ships were anchored in the bay. There were no docks or wharves. The boats from our ship landed on the beach. A delegation of citizens was standing in the sand waiting to greet us and point us to the shed where we were to register. My documents listed my name as Pedro Davila de Velazquez. The Davila brothers were not comfortable with me using their name to register. They paid the notary some money and I registered as Tomas El Huérfano.

The young men who came to the Indies were an adventurous and rough group. Some had left their homes to seek riches. Others, like me, left because of troubles. Many of them were hidalgo and were somewhat educated. There were also common men who came as servants or retainers to the hidalgos. As I have said there were a few holy men seeking to "save" the souls of the Indians. There were only twelve Christian women in Hispaniola at this time and eight of them were whores. Very busy whores if I might say so. But even so, many of the Castilians decided that they could save the souls of the Indian woman by taking them as concubines.

Each of us who registered and became citizens were given land and Indians. It seemed that the amount of land and number of Indians was based on family connections or the amount you could pay the notary. The Davilia's had paid my expenses in Cadiz and had paid my passage. I had no money and my family connections were unknown. The Davilias vouched for me and said that I was the bastard son of a noble family. They assured the notary that my family had served well in the wars to punish and eliminate the moors.

I still had Pedro Davila's sword. It was my only tool. I was given a very small plot of land and two Indian brothers named Halaso and Fodi. Their sister Koiara was also given to me. It seemed that all the Castilians was given women.

The three were to work and serve me in all things. My duty was to teach them to accept our savior.

During the next three years, these Indians would become my family and friends.

My new servants and I walked for somewhat more than two days out of the town to our new home. The older brother, Halaso, had been a leader of his tribe. He and his family had been driven from their home and had been given the cursory christening that was so common here. Many Indians were said to be "converted", even though they knew nothing about our savior and the holy church. The priests that were here said a few words and then baptized the Indians, even though the Indians could not understand Castilian and had no idea what the Priests were saying.

Halaso said that he had a few Castilian words. But he seemed to understand things I said. We were able to communicate somewhat if not with words then with gestures. I later learned that he spoke and understood Castilian very well, but during the first weeks he pretended not to.

When we arrived at the land I had been given, I found it to be full of small trees and vines and thorns. Halaso pointed to my sword and made it known that I was to begin clearing the land. I turned and watched the woman walk away into the forest. Halaso made it clear that she would gather food for us.

My sword was of good quality steel. But it could not be used as an axe. So I began cutting the vines and the huge leaves that Halaso pointed out to me.

It was expected that Koiara would serve my carnal needs. It did not feel right for me to live like this while teaching these three souls about our lord. I tried to speak to Halaso about this dilemma, I am not sure he understood why it bothered me but he understood what I wanted. Within a month, I felt I could not live like this. We marched back to town and Koiara (her name meant deer woman) and I were married.

The local priest, Frey Olmos gave Koiara the name Cara Maria. But she will always be Koiara in my memory

Over the next year we had a happy life. We grew and sold food and cotton. We hunted and fished. We traded for tools and built a proper house in the Indian style. We worked every day and in the evenings I would teach my new family the Castilian language and they would teach me their Taino language. They would sing and sometimes dance. Halaso especially knew many songs. On the day of our lord we would not work and I instructed them in the holy teachings of our savior and his holy mother Santa Maria.

Some evenings as we sat outside, we would play games. I would perform the tricks and illusions I had learned by reading the books of the Jews. They were delighted and laughed like children when I made objects disappear and then found them again in their ears. Halaso would tell stories while prancing around and acting out the events he was telling. His stories and gestures helped me learn their language.

As I have said Halaso had been a respected and educated leader in his tribe. He had traveled around the islands of the Indies when he was young. He knew many of the other groups and their languages. He spoke often of a large island to the west. The people there, he said were rich and powerful, but also very cruel. Their gods demanded blood so they cut out the hearts of their enemies and fed the blood to their gods. He had lived with them for a few years and learned their language and knew the names of their gods. He said it would be best if the Christians did not go there because the mighty armies of these people, he called them Mexica, would kill us all.

In 1509, I felt the lessons were complete enough for my family to understand what being a Christian really meant. We walked to the town and the church where they were baptized. Koiara already had her Christian name. Halaso and Fodi had also chosen Christian names. This made it easier to keep the local holy brothers away from our farm. I could not understand why good, honest peaceful people such as these should be made to accept new names. In their lives, they lived as Christ would have wanted them to live. When we were alone we used the Taino names. I helped them understand that many of the Castilians called themselves Christian but did not live a life that Christ would approve of. I told them that to me, to Santa Maria and to the most holy, names did not matter. All that mattered was how we lived our lives.

In late April of 1510 an Indian came to our farm and told us of trouble in the south part of the island. Many of the Taino remembered the execution in 1503 when their martyr queen

Anacaona was hung. They had risen up and were raiding farms and killing settlers.

Two days later a group of Castilians led by Governor Nicolas Ovando rode up to the house. I was told that I must join a force going to punish the rebellious tribes. I initially refused to go. Ovando insisted that I go. He told me that I would be stripped of my citizenship if I did not go. He said that my Indians, even though they were now Christians, would be given to others. With that threat they rode away and said I was to meet them in the town in exactly four days.

I watched them leave and spoke to Halaso asking him to lead us all to the forest away from the Castilians. But when I said this, he refused; he said I must go, if only because I could speak the Taino language and knew their ways. Perhaps I could help save lives.

I left for the town the next day, when I arrived I told the Ovando that I would go, but I would go only to try to make peace and not to kill. He told me that when I saw the mutilated bodies of Christian settlers I would change my mind.

It was on this expedition that I would meet Florida. The other settlers and I sat in the tavern and talked while waiting for the expedition to begin. Florida was there. I had seen her before and I was curious about her. I sat down across from her and asked her what country she had come from, She looked at me and spat. She asked if I wanted to hire a woman. I laughed and said I was married but that I was a student of the world and its people. She also laughed again and began to tell me her story. She said she from Abyssinia, descended from the Queen of Sheba, and had been a Christian and a Queen in her country before the Turks kidnapped her into slavery. She was large and as strong as most of the soldiers. She always carried a long dagger in her skirts. One of the huge war dogs, Negruzco, would not leave her side. Her complexion was very dark, her hair long and tangled and curly. Her face had been scarred by a blade. She made it clear to me and to the others who were listening, that she killed the man who had scarred her face and wore his shriveled privates around her neck for many months afterwards.

Whores that follow the army are not beautiful woman, but in my slight experience I had never seen one as unattractive as Florida. However, she was apparently very popular among some of the men. I also think that most of us were a little afraid of her. Besides her usual duties she had become the protector of the other woman on the island.

(Translators note: At this point several pages were damaged and unreadable or missing completely)

After the fighting stopped I was very confused about what had just happened. The Governor was right, when I saw the bodies of Castilians, bloody and mutilated, I was angry, I was furious. But mostly I was sad. I tried to understand how, and more importantly why, people could butcher each other. It was then that I understood what was called the bloodlust. On the **Dios Del Vento**, some of the men had talked about it. These men said it was an exciting feeling. They said it was as if their blood was boiling. They said it was the most alive they had ever felt. Others who were listening, who had been to war, hung their heads and said yes it was exciting but the guilt and sadness that come afterwards were not worth it.

Our little army had killed most of the Indians that we encountered, there were a few woman and children we discovered hiding. We tied them and marched back to Santo Domingo.

When we arrived back to Santo Domingo I was eager to get back to my family and farm. Governor Ovando wanted me to stay for a few days and meet the new settlers. He also said that he wanted to pay all of us soldiers. He said we would be paid in land or Indians or perhaps tools. I agreed to stay and said that I did not want more Indians but I would accept tools or more land if was adjoining my farm. He looked at me quizzically and nodded his head.

New settlers had arrived during the two months that we were gone. Every new group that arrived seemed to be more interested in gold than the group before. They did not want to farm or enjoy their new life. They wanted gold, they wanted women and slaves. They drank and bragged about the moors they had killed and the Indians they had yet to kill.

I went with some of the others, who had been in our little army, to the newly built meeting hall that served as our town center. We drank Matar al Diablo and talked to the new comers as their papers were checked and they were assigned Indians and land. I could see one of the men staring at me. He looked familiar. I thought he might be one of Vincenti's guards from Grenada. I turned away, emptied my gourd and went outside.

The Indians that would be assigned to the new comers were tied together and standing around the dock. None would look at me as I passed by them. As I left the town and walked to my home I spent many hours thinking about wars and slavery. In this new world where we had the opportunity to spread the gospel of our savior, and save thousands of innocent souls, our actions were so far from god and so close to what the Evil One would want us to do. It all began to make sense to me, evil must feed on greed. It does not matter if you are a Jew, a Moor, a heathen Indian or even a Christian, once greed seeps into your head and your blood, the great devil, enemy of our God, will come and feed on your soul.

I reached the place on the road where the path to my farm began. It appeared that no one had used the path recently. The jungle was starting to grow over it. From this point it was a short distance to my house. I brushed aside the vines and wondered why the path was not kept open. As I came to the clearing where my house sat I could see that something was wrong. The gardens had not been tended, the water gourds were empty and no one was to be seen. I called their names and then after looking around I went into the house. Halaso was there laying on his hamaca, looking very sick. I shook him and he opened his eyes and looked at me. "Where is Koiara?" I said. He coughed violently and spat vile phlegm to the ground. He turned away and said in a small voice, "Dead, they are both dead, and soon I will die also". I could not speak. I stood there staring at the wall and the ground. After a few moments I went to my knees and prayed for their souls. I got up and felt Halaso's head, he was very hot. It was a fever, a deadly fever. I had not seen it but I had heard about it. I went out. In back of the house I smelled death.

There were two shallow graves, one of them only half filled. I made the holy sign of the cross and walked by them to get water from the little stream near the house.

During the next few days in my heart I grieved for my wife and Fodi. My hands nursed Halaso. I wet his head, I gave him water and make an infusion from herbs Koiara had gathered in the months we had been happy that now seemed so long ago. I took vegetables from the garden and I trapped a bird from which I made a soup for us.

When Halaso slept, I finished the graves and made holy crosses for each of them. I was very lonely and sad. I slept very little during this time.

After four days as his fever receded, Halaso began to gather strength. Soon he was walking again and working in the garden. Our cotton field was being strangled by the jungle. I did not care. I told Halaso that as soon as he fully recovered I would leave. I said he could stay or leave as he wished.

On the tenth day, it was in November, my old friend Hernan Cortez, rode up to the house. I had known he was on the island, but I had been careful to avoid him so that no one would know my true identity. He looked down at me from his horse and said, "Tomas, I see that it is indeed you. You should have come to see me. But now there is trouble, my

88

friend, there is man in the town who says you are a murderer and heretic. He says that the Inquisition has sentenced you to death. The Governor and four men will be here tomorrow to arrest you".

"It is good to see you again Hernan, thank you for warning me, but how long have you known I was here?" I asked. He answered, "I have suspected it since you arrived, I am the notary of Azua De Compostela. I see all the papers and names. The Davila are my kinsmen. I talked to them about you. But now, if you value your life, you must go. Go to Isle de Juana. There are many souls to save there. But know this Tomas, our friendship is ended. I have helped you twice now, and if I see you again I will arrest you." With that he turned, waved his hat to me and rode off.

Halaso had been listening. He walked over to me and said, "It seems that Jesus must want you to leave Tomas, first the sickness and now this trouble. I know of sea traders who will be stopping close to us and then departing soon to trade at many islands and finally go to the land of the Totonac. They will take us with them. To the west of the Totonac there is a mighty and rich ruler I have heard of. I have seen his writings and they show that he longs for a god that is just and good and will not demand blood. He would welcome you Tomas. You can save many souls and bring Jesus and his mother to more Indians than you can image. These Totonac people are the first nation we come to on the unending land we find in the west. Best of all Tomas, there are none of your people on this big land.

I decided that I had no other choice. If I tried to leave on a Castilian ship, I would soon be discovered again and perhaps arrested. I looked up at Halaso and said, "If what you say is true, God will smile on this journey and perhaps forgive me for the lives I have taken."

I prayed at the grave of my wife and said farewell to her. We packed some food, some weapons and we set out through the jungle to the north end of the island.

In the few days that we walked I learned much about Halaso. He had been captured when he was a small boy. His captors were the Carib Indians. He had a unique talent for learning language by listening to people speak. When his captors realized this, they decided that he was a very valuable little boy. He was bought and sold several times in the next few years. At one point, before he was grown to be a man, he wound up in a city and was owned by a chief of a group he called Yukatec[12]. It was here that he was educated and taught the tales of the demons gods of the Indies. He was to become a priest, a bloodman, as I now call them. One day

---

[12] A sub group of the Maya people who live on the Yucatan Peninsula

he decided to escape. He joined a group of Merchants called Pochtecas. He became a trader and wanderer for about five years and finally came to Hispaniola and was adopted into the family of a powerful Chief. A few years later when his adopted father died, his step brother wanted to have him and other members of his family killed. It was at this time that the first Christian settlement was beginning in Santo Domingo. Halaso, Fodi and Koiara went to the settlement where Halaso quickly learned the Castilian language and became a translator. Within a few years he discovered how cruel the settlers were. He began to act dumb and said that he had forgotten many words. The settlers punished him and it was then that I arrived and was given him and the others as my slaves.

I felt truly blessed to have a man of his skill and knowledge helping me. I would be long dead if it were not for Halaso

On the fourth day we stopped at a small bay. A farm or village had recently been burned nearby. We built a hut and on the next morning Halaso told me to wait on the beach near the hut. He said was going to hunt for food and find a beacon that he remembered at the top of a mountain near the bay. He said he hoped to return in five days. He told me that if I met any Indians I was to say "Yokokatlakatl[13]

---

[13] I am a friend – Taino Language

91

Halaso". With that he took his stone knife and the iron headed spear we had made and walked off into the jungle.

I lay awake that night wondering what I would do if Halaso did not return. I worried about what would happen if a Castilian ship entered the bay. My head was full of worries. At the darkest hour of the night I tried to remember the holy mother and the blue light that surrounded her. Finally I slept. The birds and the animals of this land woke me before dawn, their calls and whistles and songs were full of life and conversation. I awoke with them.

On the second day, shortly after dawn, I saw a fire and smoke on the top of the mountain where Halaso said he was going. I fished in the bay and ate the food we had brought with us as I watched. The fire burned and smoked for four days.

On the fifth day, Halaso appeared, coming out of the jungle carrying several small animals. He greeted me and asked if I had seen anyone or any boats in the bay. I told him I had seen nothing. He said we must wait longer. The smoke continued for the next two days and then, just at dusk a very large canoe, rowed by perhaps 25 Indians came into the bay. They landed on the sand and pulled the boat up above the high tide. Halaso stood watching, his arms out, his palms open, chanting a song that I had never heard him sing. The

Indians from the boat greeted him, first bowing with their heads to the ground and then laughing and talking as if they had all been best of friends at some time in the past.

Halaso called me over, he pointed to me and, I suppose, introduced me to the Indians. The all bowed to me and watched every move I made, talking among themselves as if I were some very odd creature. Halaso told me that they were very wary of me, because the only Castilians that they had seen or heard of were cruel haughty men, who treated them like animals.

We cooked and ate dinner and afterwards they talked, sang and some danced. Some drifted off into the night but most of them lay in the sand around the fire and slept.

Early the next morning ten of the Indians unloaded two bales of cloth and marched into the forest. Just after dark they came back to the beach with a bundle of bright feathers, feathers of such beauty as I had never seen before. Halaso sat next to me and said," they have made the trades they wanted to make, in the morning we will leave."

As I have mentioned, I am not a person comfortable in boats and the sea. The center of the kanowa[14] held the trade

---

[14] Canoe

goods, mostly bundles of cloth and other things such as the feathers. My place was on top of the bundles facing the back of the boat. There were fiber ropes and cords that held me in place. At times I worried that I might be another trade commodity. I wondered what my value would be. Halaso helped with the rowing. After three days I told him that I too could row.

He agreed and I was given an Indian partner whose place I would take while he slept and ate. On the fourth day we came to an island and landed on a beach. The traders went out to the jungle with one commodity and came back with another. This sailing and trading from island to island went on for a very long time.

One day Halaso came to me and said that the Indians were ready to go home. He said we should prepare for several days at sea.

On the fourth day, after we had begun the trip to the Indians home, the color of the ocean changed. The Indians pointed to the east and seemed concerned. Halaso told me that we must row fast to beat the storm that was coming. During the next day the boat moved very quickly, all of us rowed as hard as we could without stopping for rest or meals. Near dawn of the fifth day the chief of the boatmen brought a type of rope to us and told Halaso that we all must tie ourselves together and to the boat. We managed to string the ropes and tie ourselves in and then all at once the storm was on us. The torrential rain came in from the east. It was not falling from the sky but riding the winds and the waves straight at us. We could not see ahead of us. We rode the waves as best we could. I only remember being very wet and holding on tightly while trying to hear the chief tell us how to row with the waves. There were several times that we seemed to be completely underwater. We always came up, until one time I felt I was upside down I could see the Indians around me struggling to cut their ropes, I reached for my dagger and cut my rope and grabbed a bundle of our cargo that seemed to be floating in a direction that I thought was up. Through the waves I could hear the Indians yelling. I saw Halaso once besides me. He reached to give me a piece of rope, I grabbed it and then a wave came down upon us and he was gone. I floated to the surface again and managed to tie the bundle to my chest before the next wave hit. My only memory of what came next is waking that night floating in the sea tied to a bundle. There were stars in the sky, the storm had moved on. I remember looking up and suddenly I saw a star moving very fast towards the west. I had seen the traveling stars before but this was bigger and brighter and seemed faster than others I had seen. I tried to imagine what it might be. But I was very cold and I think I must have fallen asleep again.

1511 The Messenger from God

I awoke on a sandy beach. I felt as if all my strength had been expended. I was hungry and thirsty. I did not want to move. But as I opened my eyes I could see that the sun was in the sky just a little above the horizon in the east. There was a huge eagle standing in the sand close to me. I could feel the tide washing around me. I remembered the storm. I sat up and looked around for Halaso and the others. I saw no one from the boat. But I did see a group of Indians walking out of the forest towards me. As I watched them approach, my first impression was that they were very different from the Indians I had known on the other islands. Their clothing and headdresses were more elaborate. They wore feathers and shining cloth of kinds and colors that I had never seen. They had pendants with metal or wooden images hanging from their shoulders and waists. Some had war clubs and spears. I thought, these must be the Totonac. I stood up and held my arms out and opened my hands palms face up in the peaceful gesture I had seen among the Indians. I called out to them the word I had learned that meant friend. "Yokokatlakatl!" I said in a voice as loud as I my nearly expended strength could manage. I know now that my weak voice and my poor knowledge of their speech caused them to think I was saying "Ketsalkoatl[15]" which is the name of the son of God whose messenger I was to become. As I stood there, there was a very sharp earthquake. The shaking caused the eagle to rise up and then land again. When it landed it turned to face to Indians and spread its wings. It showed no fear. It walked towards the Indians, making an odd threatening sound. Trying, I think, to scare them away from me, its potential meal just washed in from the sea. The Indians stopped and went to their knees. I looked down and saw that I was wrapped with long seaweed. The feather bundle had washed up beside me and split open, spilling the wonderful, but wet, feathers all around me. I said "Yokokatlakatl" again. They looked at the bird and then back at me and said "Ketsalkoatl tlalteuctli[16]". At that moment I noticed Halaso standing behind me. "They think you are a holy man" he said. "Stand tall and appear proud as if you were their lord". The eagle still stood, with its wings extended, between the Indians and I.

Halaso spoke to them in what I later learned to be Nahuatl, he told them to stand. He said that Ketsalkoatl's messenger,

---

[15] A god of that was worshiped in many guises throughout Mesoamerican. He was also known as Quetzalcoatl, the Feathered Serpent. Many of the myths surrounding Ketsalkoatl tell us that he was against human sacrifice. His brother Tezcatlipoca killed him and his spirit disappeared across the eastern sea with a promise to return one day as a savior.
[16] A Nahuatl word meaning "Our Lord".

meaning me, had come from the eastern sea and wanted food and water.

They stood and the eagle flew off. They exchanged more words with Halaso who told them that I was such a holy man I would not speak directly to them. Speaking among themselves, they bowed to me, gave us water, and said that they would take us to their city and give the hospitality suitable for beings such as ourselves. We then followed them into the forest and on to a road, passing by villages and farms. During this short journey I attracted much attention and must have been quite a spectacle for the people we met, they gathered round bowing and chanting as we passed. Halaso told me not to look at anyone and to face forward and have no expression. He said that when we met their leader he would bow and address that person as Tlatoani or Great Lord, when this happened I should not bow, I should look at that person and nod twice.

The Indian city we came to, Cempoala was its name, was much bigger than any I had seen before in the Indies. It was about the size of Salamanca[i].[17] It was a beautiful place. In the middle of the city, three rivers came together before flowing into the sea. The white stone buildings were tall and some were painted red or blue. They were made in shapes

---

[17] Roughly 24000 inhabitants

and forms I had never seen. They were decorated with fantastical carving.

Halaso and I were taken to a Palace. We were washed by six maidens and given white robes to wear. On the beach Halaso had repacked, picked up and carried the sodden bundle of feathers to the city. He told the maidens to lay them out to dry and comb them. He told them that they belonged to the god. They bowed deeply and took the feathers and then led us to a huge table laden with fruits and foods I could not identify. We were told to eat and to rest. While we were eating, three of their priests came to watch. Halaso went to talk to them. He pointed at me and then at the sea. They already knew about the appearance of the comet during the night and about the earthquake and the eagle. He later told me that he told them that I was the messenger of a powerful god. These were the first of many priests I would meet over the next years. I shall call them the bloodmen. The expressions on the faces of these bloodmen remind me of Frey Vincenti and some of the other inquisitors I had known. Even though, at the time, I could not understand their words I knew they were dour and humorless men. They wore black robes that were encrusted with blood. Their long hair was matted with blood. They smelled like death. I could tell they were arguing and Halaso was losing. I stood up and in my deepest most fearsome voice loudly told them to be gone. I remembered some gestures I had learned from the

Inquisition courts. I raised both hands above me, with one finger pointing towards the sky. I slowly lowered my hands towards the bloodmen. Halaso suddenly stopped talking to them. He curiously looked at me and moved away. He yelled at them and then looked at me and said, "I told them you would kill them. Say something else in your language that sounds threatening ". I loudly cursed them and as my arms moved down with the fingers pointed towards them, they ran out of the building.

I was at a great disadvantage during the period after we landed and over the next 5 years as I learned the Nahuatl language. Halaso did the talking and most of the thinking. He was always careful to explain to me what was said by others and how and why he responded. He created the basis for what was to become my great mission, the task the holy mother had given me during that holy night in the university. I was to be the agent in turning these Indians away from worship of their blood drinking gods and helping them to understand that just one loving and forgiving god watched over us all.

After the bloodmen ran off, we laughed and ate and drank as much as we were able. When we finished and pushed away from the table, we were led away to sleep and rest. The sun was high in the sky the next day when we were awakened by a messenger from the lord of Cempoala. The Lord's name was Xicomecoatl. We were escorted to his palace and then inside to his throne room. He was a very jolly and fat man. Had it not been for his Indian finery and decoration, he would have reminded me of one of the brothers who raised me in Grenada.

Halaso bowed with his face to the ground. Earlier he had told me not to bow, but to make a speech in Castilian and to smile and slowly nod twice. After bowing Halaso told the lord that I honored him and that my master the God Ketsalkoatl was happy with him and he would be soon rewarded. Halaso told him that we must go to Texcoco to see the Tlatoani Nezahualpilli. Xicomecoatl implored us to stay. Halaso said we would return and tell the Totonacs how to worship the one true god that was coming. He said now that I heralded God's coming, the old gods would be banished when the next cycle of years began. Several of the bloodmen were there and they protested. But the lord quieted them. He told Halaso that his people needed protection from the Mexica. He said that the Mexica had brought ruin on his people and they took many of the strongest young men to Tenochtitlan to be sacrificed to the gods. He told Halaso that he wished the Ketsalkoatl would free his people. Halaso nodded and told the lord that there would be no more blood sacrifice when our god, Ketsalkoatl and his father came. Xicomecoatl thanked me for coming to his city and said that he would arrange for his men to guide us to Texcoco. He then clapped his hands and three maidens appeared bearing gold jewelry and soft clothing. The lord asked me to accept the gifts, which included one of the girls who was one of his daughters. After Halaso translated all this, he said that I should accept it all, even the girl. When I told him that I could not take the girl, he thought for a moment and then told me to go over to her and examine her closely, looking especially into her eyes. I did as he asked and then asked him what to do next. He nodded and told Xicomecoatl that the girl was very special and her eyes showed the stars. He asked me again if I was sure I did not want the girl. When I told him yes, be bowed to me and to the lord. He said, "The messenger has told me that this girl will be loved by the god and taken as his daughter." He told Xicomecoatl "You must keep this girl and educate her so that she will be ready for her great father when he comes. Now we must leave in great haste. We are on business from the god. Women will slow us down. Because of the favors you have shown us, the one god will smile upon you and deliver you from your oppressors." Xicomecoatl stood up and said that our escort was waiting and we could go.

When we left the palace there was a group of warriors led by a Captain. The Captain stood next to a litter that I was supposed to lay in. In the New World there are no horses or mules. The only transport, besides walking, consists of litters carried on the shoulders of men. I would not be carried. It caused them great consternation, but Halaso and I convinced them that I would walk.

It was a long journey that eventually led up a high and cold mountain road. During the walk, Halaso was continuously telling me what I must do, how to walk and talk. How I must display nobility. I told that him this was not the way of our lord Jesus and he replied that we must be careful and gain powerful friends before we could talk of Jesus.

Before we began the climb up into the mountains, the land and the villages we passed all seemed to be fertile and prosperous. Many people came to greet us as we marched along. They brought gifts of fruit and other foods to us. In four days we came to the city known as Cholula [18]. Cholula was even larger than Cempoala. There are huge snowcapped mountains beyond this city. These mountains are considered sacred places. To match these mountains, the Cholula people built a massive man-made stone mountain temple in their city. Later I would see many of these mountain temples but this one was truly a thing of wonder. I talked to Halaso about this structure. He told me stories of the city and the gods and said that Cholula was a very old and very sacred place. From his descriptions and stories I imagined that the Indians saw Cholula as we would see Rome or perhaps

---

[18] Near the Modern city of Puebla

Jerusalem. I longed to learn more, but he said that it would be dangerous for us to stay too long in one place. No one was quite sure exactly who or what we were. The bloodmen were threatened by us. The news they had heard of who we said we were and why we were there was seen as an affront to their profession and to the other gods.

The high priest of Ketsalkoatl in Cholula would not see or meet with us. But there were groups in the city who were sympathetic. One group of nobles took us into a palace and gave us a wonderful feast. They told us that for many years they had been waiting for Ketsalkoatl to arrive and end the blood sacrifice.

Their leader said that there were many people, nobles and priests in the land who felt as they did and would follow our teaching. He confirmed what Halaso had told me. He said we were wise to go to the ruler of Texcoco. He was one who would be sympathetic to our teaching. Then one of the others warned us that the Mexica had sent warriors who were waiting on the road and would take us to Tenochtitlan. He said we should not go there. He said we should leave by night and take the northern road from Cholula, and go straightaway to Texcoco.

When we left the feast, Halaso explained this warning to the Captain of our escort. He seemed very concerned and said we should leave immediately. So without sleep, during the darkest hours we left Cholula.

After four days of walking in the high cold mountains we looked down to the huge valley of Anahuac. We looked down and saw several fine beautiful cities, great dark lakes and fields and orchards. In the middle of these lakes we looked down upon the City of the Mexica. It was a wondrous sight.

In two more days we finally began walking down and soon met warriors from Texcoco who had been sent to escort us to see their Lord. The captain of these warriors arrived with great ceremony accompanied by many guards and attendants. He was carried on a litter. He welcomed us to the land of the great Tlatoani Nezahualpilli, all the while addressing us by the title of "Tueles". He said that the Great Lord wished to see us and to tell him about the powerful god that was coming. Halaso later told me that Tueles meant that were we sort of minor gods – perhaps like angels.

I longed to begin preaching and teaching these people, but Halaso said we needed to wait and solidify our status.

About one league from the city, Nezahualpilli himself, came with a grand entourage to greet us. He was a fine looking man, perhaps fifty years of age but with a body and visage still strong. He came down from his litter and said he had

105

been waiting for us all his life. He only wished that his father, Nezahualcoyotl, had been alive to see us and meet us. I later learned that the father Nezahualcoyotl had been the wisest and greatest king ever to have lived in all these fine cities of the Indies. He was to them as Solomon is to us. He was a poet, a great judge, a wise leader and a holy man.

Nezahualpilli welcomed us and said that he looked forward to talking to us in his palace the next day. He would have his most learned scholars and priests attend and we could explain to them what the great God wanted them to do in order to prepare for his coming. He walked with us into the city and pointed out the structures and temples. At one of the great palaces he took his leave and told us that his servants would care for us and feed us until we could meet again in the coming day. We went into the palace to the same kind of ceremony and service we had received in Cempoala.

My dear reader, I must interrupt these remembrances. I am writing this story of my life in a Palace in Tenochtitlan. Many things are happening in the city and I fear that soon my wife and I may need to leave very quickly. Hernan Cortez and his army of Castilians and Tlaxcalans[19] will soon be

---

[19] Tlaxcala was a city state northeast of Cholula (modern Puebla). Tlaxcala had maintained semi-independence and hostility towards the Mexica. They fought and lost several battles

here. The Mexica nobles have been meeting to discuss what actions they should take. But the great Moctezuma[20] remains undecided. Those nobles and priests who have been converted to the one God are either keeping silent or regretting their choice. Seeing the false Christians with their greed and violence has discouraged them. My enemies, the bloodmen, are blaming me for confusing Moctezuma and angering the demon gods. So as I continue to write I shall skip many of the details of the last ten years and try to explain how I came to the position I now find myself. If we survive I will rewrite those details that I feel will provide extra clarity to my story.

And so I continue.

The day after we arrived in Texcoco, Halaso and I were led to the Palace of the lord of that city, Nezahualpilli. There were many nobles and bloodmen present. After the lord ceremoniously welcomed us, he said that his priests and nobles wished to ask me questions. Halaso seemed somewhat concerned, but after each question, he would bow to me and translate. Then he would tell me what the response should be and ask me to say a few things so that it

---

with Cortez and finally made peace and became allied with the Spanish. An unknown numbers of Tlaxcalan (at least many thousands) accompanied Cortez and were, along with smallpox, the deciding factor in his final defeat of the Mexica

[20] Moctezuma was the ruler, the Tlatoani of the Mexica.

would seem that he was translating my words. Most of the questions had to do with my knowledge of their gods, especially Ketsalkoatl. Halaso, having been educated in these tales, was able to convince the Lord and many of the others there that I, indeed, was a messenger from the god. I was not happy to find that I was representing an idol or perhaps a demon, but Halaso soon convinced me that I was mistaken.

It was here that I met my second wife, Quetzalxochitl. Besides my wife she has been my teacher and my friend. She is the niece of the present Lord of Texcoco and the Granddaughter of the Lord Nezcahualcoyotl. She was the most powerful woman in the city. and well known by other nations in this land. It was said that she can see things in the sacred polished stone mirrors that are common in their temples. It it said that she can see the future. Besides being my wife and teacher, she would be the real force and my inspiration in converting these Indians to leave their demon gods and trust in the one true God.

She was present during that first interview in the palace. After listening to Halaso's answers to the many questions, she came forward and said in words we now both remember," I have seen this messenger come from across the eastern sea, coming from that holy place atop a comet. All that his servant has told us is true. The time is coming when the fifth sun[21]will be upon us. Our gods are old; their thirst of blood has them made weak. Ketsalkoatl had journeyed far across the seas and heavens and had found the one God who is strong and rules time and all things in the heavens. The messenger is here to prepare us for the coming of Ketsalkoatl and his Holy Father. The messenger is here to help us lay the carpets for our saviors' arrival. My grandfather, our great teacher and speaker of truth and knowledge, told us that the fifth sun was coming. He told us the old gods were dying. He prepared us for the messenger. He created our gardens and our library for the time when Ketsalkoatl would come to save us and give us a peaceful home here on the earth and a new life in Heaven."

It was a speech that left some of those in the room ready to learn from me and prepare. Most of the bloodmen and many of the nobles were, however, not ready to give up the old gods and the sacrifice of blood that these so called gods demanded. But the lord Nezahualpilli ruled and demanded that they all should consider our words. He said that for now, there would be no changes. Halaso and I were Tueles and must be protected and respected by all.

---

[21] The Mexica view of the universe is that it had been created and destroyed four times. The believed that the new era of the fifth sun would result in the destruction of the world and bring a new god or gods to rule them

The next few years went by quickly. Quetzalxochitl and I grew to love one another and were married in the tradition of the Texcoco nation. Halaso and my wife taught me the Nahuatl language and with Halaso's help I taught my language to Quetzalxochitl. We would hold services each week where I would deliver sermons and lessons about Jesus and his holy mother. Halaso and Quetzalxochitl were there to help translate before I became fluent in Nahuatl. I would try to discuss the holy book but since there were no copies here it was very difficult. Our congregation of believers did not increase much during these first years. The blood sacrifices continued.

After I learned to read the picture writings of this land, Quetzalxochitl and I would go to her Grandfathers library and she would help me understand many things I had never considered. I learned that this land had a long history and that there had been many nations and many peoples. The belief of the old gods was a constant in this history although there were variations and minor changes in names and the legends. I could see that there were many similarities in the history of the old world and in the history of this new world.

One day after a long walk in Palace gardens, we touched on a startling idea. What if Jesus was not the only son of God? What if God had sent a savior to other parts of the world, so as to reveal himself to other peoples in a way they could understand and was consistent with their history? Halaso, Quetzalxochitl and I spent many, many hours discussing this idea and finally, I agreed. A loving god would not leave a whole new world without a savior of its own. He would not depend on greedy false Christians to spread his name. So my teaching, my mission suddenly became attuned to these native people and their history.

Our following in the nobility and among the common people increased greatly as we preached and taught in a way that was consistent with their lives and the stories they had learned and grown up with.

Halaso became our missionary. He would go the many cities and nations and tell them about the new age and the new God that was coming to save them.

The old picture books sometimes told conflicting tales of Ketsalkoatl, but as I read and considered all the variations I came to several conclusions. He was said to have had a virgin birth, he preached love and peace, he was against human sacrifice and he was betrayed by his brother. After his death he went to a paradise like place and told his people that he would return someday to rule over the world and give peace to all the people in the land. I began to believe and know that Ketsalkoatl was a son of God, who had been sent to be the savior of all these lands so far across the seas from the world I grew up in.

I became accepted as a priest of Ketsalkoatl. Nezahualpilli gave me the temple dedicated to this Christ of the New World. We removed the blood and the altars of death. We erected an image of Ketsalkoatl holding a cross and praying to Heaven

The bloodmen and many others were very angry. The nobles who were among my flock formed a military order whose goal was to protect me. It was called the Order of the Quetzal.

Halaso sent seekers of truth from other cities and nations in the land to come and learn from us. Even the Great Moctezuma had come to listen to us. Afterwards we met this ruler of the Mexica and spoke for many hours. I found him to be an intelligent educated man. But a man whose position was defined by a proud imperial tradition that made abandoning his old gods very difficult. But I could see that as he left, after our discussion, he was troubled and did not really understand what he should do next.

Many in our flock of believers were becoming missionaries. Halaso organized them and sent them to far parts of the land to spread this new gospel of one God and his son. I knew that some had become martyrs. But some were bringing new believers. Soon the demons were be banished and this New World would be God's land and the people would be God's people.

One day Quetzalxochitl told me said she had looked in mirror and seen that the future was uncertain. She still believed in the power of prophesy with the obsidian mirrors. The mirrors told her that my hopes may be realized but she had also seen a future of the destruction of everything in her world and the death of more people than there were stars in the sky

One day an ambassador from Cempoala came to me saying that other Tueles had arrived on the eastern shore. After his description I knew that Castilians had finally come to this land and I worried that they would bring their greed and slavery with them. Halaso, Quetzalxochitl and I tried to decide what we should do. One morning as we weighted our options, a representative from Moctezuma came to us. He was summoning us to come to him and advise us about these new Tueles who were in Cempoala.

We went to Cacamatzin the new Tlatoani and lord of Texcoco to ask his permission. Nezcahualpilli had died five years before. Cacamatzin was now a direct vassal of Moctezuma. He told us to go quickly and give advice and counsel to the great Mexica lord. He ordered that an imperial barge be made ready to take us across the lake in great ceremony.

Within a few hours we arrived in Tenochtitlan. If I had more time in writing this account, I would describe this wondrous place. It was truly the imperial capital of many nations and cities in this land. The streets and canals were full of people from all parts of the new world. There were warriors, merchants and nobles who were carried in litters, with large numbers of servants following them and carrying their goods and baggage. The markets were full of food and goods of such variety as I had never seen. I must say that the city was larger, grander and probably cleaner than Venice, Constantinople, Rome or any of the cities in the old world that I had heard or read descriptions of. But where ever we went in the city, always looming above us was the great temple of the war god Huitzilopochtli[22]. The human sacrifices to this demon god from atop this mountain like temple continued almost constantly. I had seen this abomination in Texcoco but not on the scale that we saw it here.

We would not be carried in the custom that was expected. We met our escort of Mexica at the dock and walked to the Palace of the great Lord of the Mexica.

---

[22] The Mexica war god, he was considered far more thirsty for blood than the other gods. It has been estimated that there were thousands of sacrifices every year.

When we arrived at his palace we went directly to his throne room where he began to tell us what he knew about the Castilians. These new Tueles, as he called them, were tearing down the idols and images of the old gods and killing those who would not convert. He told us that there were monsters with the Tueles, some of them part man, part huge deer, and others were huge drooling beasts that could tear a man apart. He said that they also could bring thunder and hurl lightning that killed men.

He asked who they were and why, if they were Tueles like myself, would they kill people who peacefully greeted them. I said something to the lord that may have damned my soul. I told him that they were from the land of the one God, but they had fear in their hearts and did not know that the one God and his son were here and teaching the people to believe. I refrained from saying that they were greedy and violent and they would spread death and slavery. I refrained from telling him that they should be driven from his land. Had I told him these things perhaps much of the blood and death that followed would have been avoided.

During the next months, Lord Moctezuma sent delegations and spies to watch and report. They returned with paintings and drawings. The interactions and translations between the Castilians and the Mexica were difficult. There were at least three languages and two people involved and I imagined that words were changed and twisted. I realized how lucky I was to have Halaso by my side in the early years before I could speak and understand Nahuatl.

It appeared that my countrymen were following the same pattern that they had shown on the islands, throwing down the altars and the images of the native gods without a real explanation and teaching of Christianity. They kill, lie and make war to suit their needs. But because many of the nations they have so far encountered hate the Mexica, Cortez has been able to ally with several of them, including my friends the Totonacs in Cempoala.

I decided that I needed to tell Moctezuma the truth and so I attempted to speak to him again but I could not get an audience.

From what rumors we heard, the lord was uncertain of what to do. On one day he would tell his generals to wipe the strangers out. On the next day he would say that they must be the Tueles, the angels, who were bringing the new god for of the New Age – the age of the 5th Sun. During this period of uncertainty we were ordered to stay in Tenochtitlan. We continued to hold our services and teach the ways of peace, but the nobles and the priests who attended asked many questions and we could tell that the actions of my countrymen were confusing everyone. It was during these uncertain days that I began writing this story of my life.

One day Cuitlahuac, the lord Moctezuma's brother, called us to his palace. He said that we were to go to the strangers who would soon be in Cholula. He told us they were intending to come to Tenochtitlan soon. He said that since we could speak to them directly without translators, Halaso and I were to go and see for ourselves who they were and what they wanted. I told him that I would need my guards and others to accompany me. I said that I now believed that these men were from the old gods and they would kill me.

The next day Halaso and I along with my guards and several of the Pochtecas[23], who were observers sent by Cuitlahuac, were assembled and left for Cholula.

Cholula is, as I have said, the sacred center of this land. It is the home of the great temple of Ketsalkoatl. I had many adherents in the city. The bloodmen with their twisted version of Ketsalkoatl remained in control of the temple. But he who had become the lord of Cholula, Tlaquiach was my friend and a follower of the one God. He told me that he would soon remove the old bloodmen and give me the temple for the new God. Because this city was so sacred, it was still

---

[23] A class of Traveling merchants who also acted as spies for the Mexica

independent from the Mexica. It was a place of peace and it had a very small army.

When we arrived in Cholula the Castilians were already there. I was dressed in the regalia of a priest of Ketsalkoatl. Halaso went ahead with several others to announce my approach.

The Castilians were wary, but our group was small. They were surprised by Halaso speaking their language. The Castilian officers told him that they would welcome a visit from a representative of the great king of the Mexica.

I walked into their camp and recognized several of them. Since some of the them knew that I was a fugitive I was somewhat nervous. I walked up to Cortez. I bowed and said, "Hello Hernan, It is a pleasure to see you again". The onlookers at the camp were dumb struck that an Indian Priest would speak Castilian. Cortez looked at me closely and said, "Ah Tomas, I see you have been busy. Have you become a demon worshipper?" The soldiers and officers in the camp all began talking at once, looking and pointing at me. I saw the whore, Florida with the dog, Negruzo, by her side. She smiled and winked at me. Some of the others were not as welcoming. Alvarado and others yelled that I was a heretic and murderer and I should be arrested. He began to step forward and draw his sword. Cortez quieted them and motioned for Alvarado to back away. I bowed again to Cortez and said that I needed to speak privately with him and perhaps the Padre De la Merced, Bartolome de Olmedo.

He called to Olmedo and we walked away from the others. When we were alone I told them, "I have lived in Texcoco for nearly ten years. I have learned their language and their customs. The grandfather of the present lord king was a holy man. He did much to do away with demons and the sacrifice of men. He built a temple to the one God. He called this God, the "unknowable". I now know his God is our God, There are many learned men in Texcoco and some in Tenochtitlan who are working to overthrow the idols and demons. But, Hernan, it will take a little more time. As we learned with Jews and Moors in Castile, people cannot be forced to accept Jesus and our Holy Father, they must find first them in their hearts. You cannot bring Jesus to these people by warring with them. Let Father Olmedo and the other priests help me teach them. Give them time. The Mexica lord king is confused because you have come. You have been throwing down their idols killing their priests and magicians. You cannot convert them like this. They think I am one of their Prophets who has journeyed to the east and has brought back news of a new god and a savior who is more powerful than their old idols. Hernan I beg of you let them continue to change in their hearts. Wait here and do them no more harm. I will explain to the king, the nobles, and their learned

119

men that you come to teach and not to kill. If you follow my advice, then the Mexica will invite all of you to their city and you will be like brothers to them".

Olmedo nodded I could tell he was sympathetic. He looked at Cortez and said" Captain, this is the same advise I have given you. Please consider what Tomas has said." Cortez turned from Olmedo and looked at me like I was insane. He said that I had become one of them. He said that he and his soldiers and the holy brothers with them could not tolerate the sight of the idols and demons. He said that they would convert them all or die trying. He then came closer to me and looked straight into my eyes. "Tomas my old friend, have you seen the gold? Do you know where it is stored?" "Yes" I said, "but they don't value gold like we do. They make beautiful things with it but that's really the only value that it has to them". He smiled and said, "They won't mind giving us more of it then. But we cannot wait here long or we will lose our advantage. We must be ruthless in tearing down the demon idols and killing those who oppose us. We must show them that we cannot be defeated. Do you oppose us Tomas?" There was a pause as he looked at me, "I hope not, I need you as a translator. You are a subject of our King, and, I hope, a Christian. As Captain General and as his Majesty's representative I order you to go back to Lord Moctezuma and tell him we are his friends. Our King, who is now their King and lord, loves him and tells him and his people to accept our savior now without delay. Tell him he must tear down the idols and stop the sacrifices and tell him we need gold and beautiful things to take to the King. We will stay here for five days. If we don't hear from you, we will come to the city. Do this and you will be pardoned" I shook my head and told him he was making a big mistake that would only result in blood, blood of Castilians and blood of Indians. I told him to remember that our lord had said, "Blessed be the peacemakers". Olmedo made the sign of the cross

With that I turned and walked off to my guards. Hernan called after me, "Remember who you are Tomas, I could arrest you now. If you oppose us I will personally kill you as if you were one of the demons".

The Pochtecas were mingling with the soldiers and looking at their supplies and clothing. The war dogs were leashed but growling and lunging at the Mexica as they walked about. I called to the Pochtecas, we gathered and I told them what had happened. They met privately and sent fast runners back to the city.

I later learned that Cuitlahuac sent a large group of warriors to ambush and kill the Castilians before they could come to the city. When Cortez heard about this ambush from the Tlaxcala spies, he and his army killed thousands of defenseless believers and nearly all the nobility of Cholula. It was a pointless act. Many of these people had already abandoned the blood gods and believed only in the one true God of peace and life.

Moctezuma sent for Cuitlahuac and demanded to know why he had tried to kill the Tueles as he called them. Cuitlahuac fearing for his life blamed the massacre on my followers. Later that day the great lord's nephew came to me and said that Halaso, Quetzalxochitl and I were not to leave the palace until he ordered. It was then that we began to fear for our lives.

I have now come to the present day in this accounting of my life.

Today[24] Cortez, his soldiers and over one thousand Tlaxcalan warriors entered the city.

On this the seventh day since the arrival of my countrymen, we are hearing reports that the Lord Moctezuma is a prisoner. He tells the people that he lives as a guest of the Tueles. When he walks in the city now, he is always accompanied by Castilian soldiers. He does not return to his palace. He stay with Cortez in the mansion where the

---

[24] Translater's note: Tomas later scratched off the word "today" and replaced it with a date – November 8, 1519

Castilians have taken residence. I am certain that Cortez is holding to him as a hostage.

Translators note: Some of the following pages have smeared and the paint or ink used to write has faded almost to the point of invisibility. I will make a note when a passage is unreadable and if a passage has a meaning that I can ascertain I will fill in words that I believe convey the intended meaning. These words will be italicized and underlined. If I cannot determine any possible intentions or meanings to words or passages, I will indicate where they sit in the manuscript by the following "..................".

Two months have passed since Cortez entered the city. There is intrigue and gossip everywhere but no one will act without orders from their captive Lord.

Frey Olmedo has visited us several times. He says that Moctezuma is happy and in good health and that he is studying and praying so he can learn to accept holy Jesus as his lord and savior.

Frey Olmedo also tells me that that he believes it to be the fourth day of the year 1520. I shall begin to count the days and date my book, *which has now become a* record of events as they are happening.

January 9, 1520

Our friends in the city visit us and yesterday told us that Moctezuma has **given Cortez** the treasure that belonged to his father. I worry that this act may greatly increase the greed of my countrymen.

Other nobles and lords such as Cuitlahuac and Cacamatzin had **tried to organize** resistance, but the generals and nobility will not attack the Castilians unless ordered to by Moctezuma. When Cortez heard of this threat, **he took action**. Now Cuitlahuac, Cacamatzin and other nobles are said to also be prisoners.

The Castilians walk the streets of the City without fear. Florida, the woman I met many years ago during the war with the Indians in Hispaniola, has created a sensation as she walks with the war dog Negruzco. Even the bloodmen seemed mesmerized to see her. She is far taller **and bigger** than almost everyone here. Her size along with her black face and long wool like hair are causing people to believe that she and the huge slobbering dog are gods come to earth. She **once told me that she** had been a queen when she was young. Even though she is a whore in Cortez's army, she acts the part of goddess and queen when she walks the streets.

April 14, 1550

I have not written for several months. Life here continues to deteriorate. Ink **and the goat skin I use** for writing have become very hard to find.

The bloodmen have been stirring up the people and blaming The Tlaxcalans, and of course, myself and Quetzalxochitl for the chaos in city. When Moctezuma talks to the people from the roof of the palace where he remains a prisoner, he continues to claim that his jailers are the Tueles or angels from god, he never mentions us and the "One god" faith we have been teaching. Every day now mobs led by bloodmen come to our house and chant against us, **saying that the** demon god Huitzilopochtli demands our blood.

Halaso has a plan to leave the city and find one of the great armies near the Tarascan borders and convince them to come back to drive the Castilians and their allies away. He says that if they can capture horses **and learn to make** the harquebus weapons that **they will easily defeat** the invaders. He says he **will try to leave before** dawn tomorrow.

April 20 1520

About two hundred of my students and the believers that I still communicate with have come to ask us what they should be doing. There is confusion everywhere in the city. I told them that Cortez and his soldiers are enemies of the One God, no matter what they say. I tell them that Cortez has been sent by the demons and he and the **others who** follow him will kill and make slaves of all the people in **all the cities** of the land.

Translators note: At this point two pages are completely faded and unreadable

May 2, 1520
We have just received news that **Cortez and about** half of his soldiers and Tlaxcalan allies have left the city, leaving Alvarado as Captain. I have **great fear** that the greed and cruelty of Alvarado will be unchecked.

I have received no news of Halaso. He has been gone now for more than 15 days.

May 5, 1520
The festival of the demon Tezcatlipoca begins today. Quetzalxochitl has made this demon her particular enemy. She has discovered how to control his tools, the mirrors he **uses for prophesy. This diminishes his** powers. It will be a dangerous time, the demon priests hate us. Quetzalxochitl was supposed to have grown up to be a disciple and high priest of Tezcatlipoca, and now she is seen **as a traitor** and thief by the demon's priests.

There are fires and the noise from fighting now every day. The Castilians have fortified their quarters and come out only in force to look for food and water.

May 12, 1520

We have remained inside for two weeks now. Our guards have been **disappearing**. We think they have been taken by the **bloodmen.**

May 19, 1550

The last few days have been the most frightening days and ultimately the most holy days of my life. The events of these days may indeed be the beginning of a new age in the world. An age where **people of** my world, the old world across the sea, can realize that God has come to others and given them a savior just as he did in **the their world**.

I will begin describing these events starting in the evening of May 12.

During the dark hours as we slept, we awoke to a loud rumbling and shaking. We went the roof and saw flames and flashes from the fire mountains to the southeast in the direction of Cholula. These mountains were considered holy **abodes of** gods by the bloodmen. Soon there were people and torches throughout the city and around the lake. The fires atop the temples were lit and flaming high. Below we could see a group of people at the doors of our home. There were bloodmen **bellowing that** Quetzalxochitl and I were the source of the evil that had overtaken the city. They yelled that Tezcatlipoca would destroy them all if he could not drink our blood. We considered escape but our door was breached and we **could hear people** running up towards us. We knelt to pray.

Warriors came up to the roof, tied us and took us away. I tried to fight. I remember being hit on the shoulder with a macuahuitl[25]. I fell, my right arm was numb. I could hear a bloodman yelling that my blood was for the gods and I should not be killed, nor should my blood be wasted until I was at the altar. He began wrapping my arm in cloth. I looked around to see Quetzalxochitl screaming and fighting even as **she was being bound**, and then I lost consciousness.

I awoke in a room reeking of death and blood. I was tied to a stone table. There were several bloodmen **around me** painting my body. There were other tables and I looked around and recognized several of my disciples' **also being** painted. They seemed to be lying **on the tables** listless and staring blankly to ceiling.

---

[25] A weapon of the Mexica. It is a flat wood club with knives of Obsidian attached

I asked for water. I told them my blood would be too thick to drink unless I had water. I could see other bloodmen boiling water over a fire and pouring it into cups. They had placed some sort of vegetable in the cups. I remembered learning about the rituals of sacrifice. The bloodmen drugged their victims to make *it easier for them to* be killed. They held my mouth open and poured the bitter hot liquid into my throat.

I asked about Quetzalxochitl, I asked where she was. The bloodmen were standing over me chanting and drumming in a ritual language that I could not understand. One of them looked down and said the sorceress was being prepared and soon we would be together in the underworld. I laughed at him and said the underworld and eternal torture was reserved for him and all the others. I said that Quetzalxochitl *and all our* disciple's would live in paradise forever in the palace of the One God. I said the Ketsalkoatl had died and made the last *sacrifice for all of us*. They all looked down at me and began chanting again.

Soon I began to feel weightless. I forgot what was happening. I focused on the reflection of the flames dancing on the ceiling. I could see the shadow of Quetzalxochitl's face appear in the flames. I do not know how much time passed.

The next **thing I knew was being held** upright and led outside. I was on the top of Hueteocalli[26] between the two sanctuaries. A fire was burning behind me and as I looked below **I could see** thousands of people watching. There were drums beating from every direction. Bloodmen were dancing and chanting all around me. In my drugged mind I thought to myself, if I were not **bound and being held** it would be possible for me to fly away. The high priest, the leader of the bloodmen was preaching to the people. He was telling them that Tezcatlipoca wanted our blood and the blood of all the Tueles in the city. I looked around and could see Quetzalxochitl and the disciples standing tied and being held. I looked around further to my right and on the Chac Mol[27] a Castilian lay on his back his head hanging down one side and feet dangling on the other. There was a pool of blood under him running through the gutters that lie around the altar and then down to a hollow stone. The priest's words faded from my mind. I could only think of the others about to die. I tried to speak and could not. I tried to focus my mind and with great effort I finally spoke. I told my **disciples not** be afraid. I said soon we would be together in paradise. I looked at my wife and told her that our love would never end.

---

[26] This is the name of the largest Mexica temple in Tenochtitlan. Known now as the Templo Mayor. The stone from this temple was used to build the great Cathedral in Mexico City.
[27] The altar on which the sacrificial victim is laid across

Then there were new torches that suddenly leapt alive above us. It lit a horrific sight. There were two figures sitting on two momoztli[28] on a platform, about the height of a man, above us. One of the figures was what appeared to be a very large woman, her skirts was covered in writhing snakes. She had a necklace composed of body parts and skulls. I remembered a huge statue in the square beneath one of temples in the city. This woman was the personification of that statue. She was in the guise of the mother of all the demons, Coatlicue. The other figure was even more grotesque and in my still altered state it seemed to me that it must truly be a demon. Perhaps the great Satan himself, Tezcatlipoca. It was an animal but it sat upright. It's body was black and yellow stripes were painted on its face. It wore a blue feathered headdress and what appeared to be a black mirror reflecting the flames from nearby torches on its chest. One of the priests standing next to it held something to its side and it let out a huge roar. Suddenly the crowd below became very quiet. Everyone seemed to looking up to the sky.

I looked around, gray ash was falling. It was like a dry snow. The ash was so thick that, except for points of fire, the city was nearly invisible from the top of the Temple. The wind began to blow and seemed to cause the smoke cloud *above*

[28] A high stone seat the gods sit atop to view the world

us began to swirl and the forms of the demons Huitzilopochtli and Tezcatlipoca started to take shape. This did not frighten me. Quetzalxochitl told me the secret of this illusion. The bloodmen funnel light from a fire. This light goes up a flexible chimney that has mica mirrors. It has *stencils or masks at* the top. These masks make patterns in the smoke that seem like the faces of their demon gods.

The people standing below us were pointing and gesturing wildly. The demon on the momoztli roared again. I could see several of the blood priests *rushing to the side of* the temple. Those of us about to be sacrificed stood or lay silently, looking transfixed at the smoke figures above us. Many of the disciples had fallen to their knees. They were bewildered and frightened. The animal demon seemed to *float down from* the momoztli. It was attached to some sort of slab that held its body rigid. The bloodman who stood above the dead *Castilian soldier reached* down with a large stone knife and cut the leg from the soldier's body. He threw it to the animal demon. The demon roared again. Other *bloodmen threw the* body over the side of the temple.

The chief of the blood priests, Tlamocazqui, who was to perform the final sacrifices came rushing forward screaming at the *crowd* below that the gods had *returned and* wanted the blood of Quetzalxochitl, myself and the other deniers of their power. He and *the others yelled* that Ketsalkoatl was dead. He grabbed Quetzalxochitl by the hair and dragged her to the Chac Mol. The demon animal roared again and ripped itself loose from the slab it was tied to. It dropped, ran on four legs and lunged at Tlamocazqui, knocking him down and stood above him growling. The bloodmen **assisting him ran back** from the altar with terrified looks on their faces.

Then rain started to fall, the smoke demons above us quickly dissolved. Quetzalxochitl, still tied, crawled down from the altar and stood up. **The ash and rain** stopped and red rose petals began to fall all around us. A new cloud, a white cloud formed above and floated to the platform. A bright blue light illuminated the whole city. A young Mexica woman appeared in the cloud. She had an incandescent blue glow with a halo of stars around her body. Even with darker skin and Indian features I immediately recognized her. It was the holy virgin mother. One of our **young disciples**, Ocelotl, immediately called out and said it was Tonantzin Chimalma[29]. This was the name of the virgin mother of Ketsalkoatl. Could it be, I thought, the holy mother of our savior Jesus is also the mother of the savior of the Mexica?

She was holding out her arms calling to the people, telling them of her love. Even the bloodmen were on their knees

---

[29] Tonantzin means "Our Lady". Chimalma was the virgin mother of Ketsalkoatl

bowing and chanting. One of them ran to me and untied my bonds. Quetzalxochitl and the others were also untied. As they landed on the platform, the rose petals turned to a rose scented water. This rose water washed the blood and the odor of death away. **The woman dressed as** Coatlicue, who I realized was the whore Florida, came to sit below Tonantzin and pray. The animal demon which I then knew was Negruzco, the war dog, lay down in front of her. Tonantzin Chimalma held out her hands for quiet. She spoke these words; they are burned into my mind. I will never forget them. She spoke to the thousands of the Mexica, who were gathered in the sacred plaza at the base of Hueteocalli, in voice soft yet a voice that each person in the multitudes below heard and understood perfectly. These were her holy words.

"I am here, I who am your mother
Your saviors messenger came with the comet,
The messenger came from the sea
in flames and with the visage of the sun.

You knew the Feathered Serpent was returning,
You knew a new world was coming.
You did not know the old gods were leaving you,
You did not know they were overthrown.

This then is God's message, this is what he tells you:

"I am He who has set the four skies in motion.
He who turned the oceans into your blood
I am your beginning and I am your end.
You are part of me and I will be part of you.
I am He, who watches at the time of the end of all life,

Your old gods, gods of your fathers, bow to me, fear me.
These old gods are weak now,
I sent to you the messenger. I sent you my words,
I am God of your children. God of your blood forever.
The drinkers of blood will go, They will leave forever
I drink only of your faith and love.
I have more things to tell you, lessons you must learn.

Beware of the others who come from the eastern sea,
the Strangers who come to you,
They will spit your blood on the ground and drink your life.
They are the old gods disguised
They are the old gods returning to enslave you"

135

Translators note: at least one page is missing at this point

.... the next days we were overwhelmed with people coming to receive a form of baptism that I had devised. Those wishing to become disciples of the One God and the holy Mother of the Saviors of Man included many of the noble families, there were bloodmen and their assistants and there were warriors, merchants, and common people. They all came.

Translators note: Here more pages are completely faded and unreadable

The Tlatoani Moctezuma had heard about the miracle and the changes in his city. But he had not appeared **on the roof** to speak to his people **since the** visitation of Tonantzin.

On May 18ᵗʰ I assembled about two thousand of the disciples and we went to the Palace where the Castilians **were living with the imprisoned Moctezuma**. The **entrances and windows were** blocked and fortified. We stood outside and called for Moctezuma and for Alvarado. They soon appeared on the roof along with armed Tlaxcalans and guards. I asked **them to come down and** meet with us. They told me to come to them. I refused, knowing that Alvarado would arrest or kill me if he had the chance. They relented and soon

Alvarado and The Lord **Moctezuma** along with **about** 100 **of** ....guards came out. They brought the leashed dogs to intimidate us. We spoke at a distance of **....... I told** them that the sacrifices would not happen again. I told them that the city was converted from serving the demons and now believed in and served our one true god and his savior. I told him to release Moctezuma and all would be peace and friendship between us. We could trade and treat each other as independent kingdoms and **have relationships like** those Castile has with its neighbors. I told the Tlaxcalans that the Mexica would no longer take the blood and lives of their young people and that Tlaxcala and the other peoples in this land would be free of the dominance of the Mexica.

I could see that Moctezuma was angry. He spoke to me in his loudest, most haughty voice and asked who was I to be making promises like that for his people. He said I was nobody and that **I should be given up** to the gods. Alvarado told the guards to take him away and then told us that he was pleased and that the Captain General Cortez would be pleased when he returned. He said that **once we pledged our fealty** to the Holy Roman Emperor and king of Castile and Aragon, Charles V, and once we paid our tribute in gold, then **our friendship and** brotherhood would become true and bonded.

I told him that the Lord Moctezuma must be released and must consult with the nobles of the city before that could happen. Alvarado said that we could talk again when the Captain General returned. He then marched back in the palace.

The people were gravely disappointed. Many of the nobility said that these so called Tueles were our enemy as Tonantzin had told us and *that we needed to* force them to leave. I told them that all peaceful means should be exhausted before we used force. I told them that we needed to wait until Cortez returned. Quetzalxochitl and I along with our close *friends returned to our home* and planned for a great festival of our Ketsalkoatl and his Holy Mother. This festival would replace the festival for the demon Tezcatlipoca which had always happened on May 20.

May 21, 1520 – A terrible disaster has occurred. Alvarado, in his greed and fear, has killed hundreds of our most influential disciples while they celebrated and danced in the sacred plaza.

Many of these people were our friends and disciples. The blood and butchered bodies *were more than I could* stand to see. In my eyes the Castilians were just as possessed by the demons of death as the bloodmen.

The **city is now** nearly without leaders. Groups of armed people are forming everywhere. They are **screaming for Moctezuma** and for death of the **Castilians**. The remaining Tlaxcalans are said to be uneasy and are considering leaving the city. The bloodmen still loyal to the demons are telling everyone that Quetzalxochitl and I are to blame for the massacre.

May 22,1520 - Florida and the dog Negruzco have come to us. The dog was bleeding from a knife wound. Florida told us that the dog had **bitten one** of the Castilians soldiers and nearly killed a Tlaxcalan warrior. Alvarado ordered Florida and the dog chained. But last night while most of the soldiers were killing the Mexica at the Festival, one of Florida's **friends** let her **and the dog** free. During the chaos of the night they came here to us for shelter and safety.

We have cleaned and bound the dog's wounds.

Even though the dog saved her life, Quetzalxochitl is not happy to have them here. She does not trust Florida. We asked Florida to explain to us how it was that she and the dog were on the momoztli atop the Great Temple mascaraing as demons.

She told us that the dog had eaten something on the street and he collapsed. She tried to carry and drag him back, but a group of bloodmen and warriors captured her and took them both away. She says she and the dog were drugged and dressed and **painted to appear** as demons. The dog was tied, standing on his hind legs, **onto a wooden** slab. They were both carried up and placed in the momoztli. One of the bloodmen was assigned to poke Negruzco with a dagger to make him roar. He was not fed and their plan was that his hunger would make him eat the limb **of** ..... **s**acrificed

Here there are two pages that are faded badly and unreadable. I believe that a different sort of ink or paint had been used.

June 16, 1520 – The markets are in chaos now. The demon priests, the bloodmen, are the only real leadership left in the city now. It is difficult to find the ink paint I am using to write this account. We are still able to obtain food and water, but the mobs outside **our doors** threaten us. There is a rumor that Cortez may be returning to the city soon. The merchants and workers in the city are leaving with their wives and children. The Castilians go out of their fortified palace only in force and only to obtain food. Occasionally one will be captured and sacrificed to the blood gods. We have **seen canoes with** young men arriving daily. These are most likely warriors returning from the remote areas. There are rumors that a new Tlatoani has been chosen but the streets are still in chaos and no real leadership has emerged. Nearly every day the lord Moctezuma appears on the roof of the palace where he is being held. He tries to calm the population. But each time he **appears fewer** and fewer people come to listen to him.

I have tried, by way of the servants who can still come and go, to ask the newcomers to the city about Halaso. No one knows anything about him.

Quetzalxochitl and the few friends and servants we have remaining are planning our escape. We are concerned that soon the demons **may once again try to drink** our blood.

Three pages here are unreadable

June 25, 1520 – Yesterday Cortez returned with many more soldiers, more gunpowder, dogs and weapons. Our escape is still blocked. There are barricades and warriors everywhere on the streets and canals. There is a rumor circulating that Cuitlahuac has been chosen as the new Tlatoani. If this is true, the Mexica will soon attack and kill Cortez, all the soldiers and the Tlaxcalans. I am not sure I will be able to stand hearing the screams and seeing the blood of my countrymen if they are sacrificed. Many people are saying that Moctezuma should have been killed and the invaders destroyed before the reinforcement and supplies arrived. But the Mexica have blocked almost all the escape routes. I have no confidence that Cortez and the others will leave the city alive.

June 30, 1520 - Our servants came today to say the Lord Moctezuma was hit by a rock thrown by a mob listening to him. They say his head was bloody and he fell. He was carried away by Castilian soldiers. If there were any here who were still his followers, their hopes for a peaceful solution are gone. They will all rally around Cuitlahuac. I fear that the native followers of God and his holy son Ketsalkoatl will be blamed for the confusion and weakness that have left the Mexica in this situation.

One of our students and disciples, a young man by the name of Ocelotl, came to us to say that he had a canoe and a plan ready for us to escape.

1536 The discovery of this manuscript

Translators note: These last pages were written in 1536 by Tomas's adopted father Esteban Saldivar. He bound the manuscript and added the following few pages.

I, Esteban Zaldivar, Priest and father confessor of the Franciscan Order add these final pages to this manuscript.

This history of the life of my adopted son Tomas the Orphan of Grenada, was found in the year of our lord 1536 by Martin Ocelotl, a Christian Indian. It and a rolled up scroll were found during the destruction of one of the ruined palaces here in the City of the Mexica.

The manuscript sheds light on questions that I have prayed for guidance about since I arrived in New Spain. The Indians here in the City of the Mexica and the surrounding provinces are being baptized in great numbers. My dilemma involves the way this is happening. They are given a choice, they can be baptized or they can be tortured and in some cases killed, especially if they are found to be performing the rituals of the demon worship that was prevalent here before we, the bringers of salvation, arrived.

My task is to teach the Indians about our lord. My prayer and private thoughts wonder if an intelligent, civilized people such as these Indians must been, can find salvation and

143

abandon their history to believe in our lord in such a short time. All people must be taught and must find the internal light in their soul before they can achieve true salvation and belief in our Holy Lord God and his son Jesus. In the provinces of Spain we exiled and killed the Jews and Moors who would not submit to our lord and God. We are doing the same thing here in this new world. Could this be what Jesus taught us ?

During my teachings and before I found Tomas's writings, the Indians asked many questions. They told me about events that are never mentioned in accounts and histories provided by the soldiers and holy men who were with Cortez and Alvarado. They said that there was a savior here and a messenger from that savior was sent to them by God. They said that many of the Indians had abandoned the devil worship and that there had been an appearance of the holy Mother. I wondered and prayed to learn more about this. Now I have the full story written by that messenger himself, who I now know was my adopted son Tomas. Tomas taught these people that this New World can have its own salvation. He told them that with God's grace, salvation will happen in a way they can understand and it will be based on their history and their customs. This is, of course, heresy and cannot be included in the teaching of the church.

When I hear these things I must pray for the Indians and tell them that the fathers of the inquisition would punish them for such thoughts. But in my heart I wonder at the truth of it. For this understanding I pray each day.

From all the histories and spoken accounts of the soldiers of Christ and survivors of the Mexica that I have read and heard, it is apparent that this city was one of the largest and grandest in all the world. Now it is all is mud and chaos. The lakes are being drained to build a new city. The pagan Mosques[30] and buildings of the Mexica city are being demolished and the stone is being used to construct a new city of our design and under our rule. I am told thousands of the scrolls of their picture writings contain poetry and histories. These are being burned as they are found. We are destroying an entire history and identity of the people in this land. God forgive us.

Now I have this manuscript and scroll that may tell us about the visitation of the Holy Mother. I am troubled because I know that Tomas was a holy and learned man. I know he fell afoul of the inquisition and his church, but I have never doubted his belief and love for God and his son our Lord Jesus.

---

[30] The Spanish called the temples of the Indians "Mosques"

Martin Ocelotl, the Indian who gave me the manuscript, seems to be a leader of those whose beliefs I have recorded above. He is a holy man of about 30 years and he says that he personally saw the appearance of our Holy Mother and he knew Tomas and his wife very well.

He said that he had known of the manuscript but thought it had been lost when the palace burned. When the stones were being removed from the ruins of the building, he went back to look for it. He found it brought it to me. He also found the scroll. He said that he thought Tomas had it painted after the visitation. He says the scroll and manuscript are proof that Tomas was here and that the Virgin Mother appeared to the Mexica before the final conquest.

I have attempted to talk to my friend the Bishop Juan de Zumárraga_about these beliefs and told him that I wanted to show him the manuscript and scroll. He warned me not to speak of it again. He told me to burn them immediately. God forgive me, but later I told the Bishop that I had burned them. I lied to him and I have not confessed or done penance for that lie. Soon after my sin, the Bishop said that I was being sent away on a mission. It was for my own safety and salvation. I would help start a new colony in the north.

I will leave soon as Padre de Merced with an expedition led by Juan de Tolosa and Christobal Onate.

Father Esteban Zaldivar y Gomez

In the city of the Mexica, New Spain.

On May 12 in the year of our lord 1532

Part 3 Stephen

In Mexico City, on the thirty fourth floor of the hotel Nikko, Stephen stood up and looked at the rain pounding on the window. He had just finished the book. He had been reading for about four hours,. He thought it had been interesting, but he wondered about the ending. He wondered what had happened when the story suddenly stopped. The book was open to the final page written by Tomas and he read the last few pages over and over hoping to get some hint of what happened to Tomas, was he was killed or did he escape? He sat back down and as he sat there thinking, he found himself dozing off.

The time when one starts to sleep, while still reading, is very interesting. Words appear that are not in the text and sometimes it is hard to know if you are really reading or if you are dreaming.

After he decided that he really wasn't really reading, he was just dozing and looking at the words. He put the book down and closed his eyes to take a nap. He had a very strange and somewhat troubling dream during that nap. He dreamt that he was in a deep hole or perhaps a cave, it was very dark but there were flashes of light in front of him. In one of the flashes he saw something lying in a circle around him. It was like a huge snake but there were colorful iridescent plumes around it. The flashes came and went quickly like a strobe light. He felt paralyzed and couldn't move. But he managed to look up and during one of the flashes; he saw two figures in the shadows to the right. One was a small woman and another was a large animal of some kind. He heard a voice call his name. It was a voice that he knew but could not identify.

Then far away he heard a bell ringing and he woke up. It was the phone. He picked it up, completely disoriented with one part of his mind reviewing and obsessing about the images in the dream and the other part speaking into the phone. The caller was a Mexicana Airlines representative. She called to tell him that there was a good chance the nearby volcano Popocatepetl would erupt tomorrow and the prevailing winds would be covering the sky and the city with ash. All flights were on hold. She said he should check back with them the next morning. When he put the phone down he thought that he should call his wife and tell her that his trip home might be delayed again. But the part of his brain obsessing about the dream took over. It was the most vivid and clear dream he had ever experienced. The most unusual thing about it was the fact that even fully awake he remembered the entire dream very clearly. The voice that had called his name was familiar. It kept repeating in his mind and he tried and tried to remember whose voice it was.

He got up and looked out the window, there were tiny flashes of light from somewhere in the downtown area. Suddenly he realized that the voice he heard in the dream was the woman, Iuitl, whom he had met earlier. After the satisfaction of finally solving the mystery of the voice, it struck him that when he had asked Martin about how it was that she thought she could remember him even though they had never met. Martin had told him ..."She knows you from her dreams".

As he continued to look out the window, he thought, it was this odd remark that Martin made that had placed her voice in my dream. My unconscious must have been struggling with how to understand it.

He looked at his watch. It was 10:40pm, almost too late to call home. But he knew he should do it anyway. So he called his wife and explained what the airline had told him and said he would call back tomorrow to update her. They exchanged the usual news of home and family, said their "I love you's" and hung up. After he put the phone down he wondered why he didn't tell her about his day and the book. He decided that he would explain it all and show her the book when he got home.

He was tired. The nap he had taken was not a restful nap, probably because of the dream. So he showered and got into bed hoping to fall asleep. But it turned out to be one of those nights when his mind would not shut down. His thoughts were jumbled and chaotic with questions and theories of what had really happened to him. But after about four hours he finally fell asleep.

Sometime around 5:30 he woke up from another dream. He had been on one of the big temples of the Mexica. There were hundreds of people on the ground, a Mexica Priest with blood soaked and encrusted robes was about to about to kill and pull the beating heart from a man lying on his back atop an altar. Stephen remembered that he had yelled and moved to stop the priest. But no one paid any attention to him. It was like he was watching but he was invisible to everyone. He turned and saw some kind of Grotesque animal running toward him. Stephen stepped back and started to stumble down the steep steps on the side of the temple. That's when he woke up, standing at the entry to the bathroom. As he awoke he turned quickly, still not knowing exactly where he was. He ran head first into the door. He jumped back and reached up to his head and realized he was bleeding. The pain from the cut on his forehead brought him back to reality at least until he walked over to the window and opened the curtains. It was a little after dawn, In the hazy light he thought he could see the temples and palaces of the Mexica as they must have looked before the Spanish came and tore them down. Looking down he saw hundreds of people in brightly colored native clothing looking up at him. All this happened in just a few seconds. He heard something behind him and quickly turned around looking back at the dimly lit room. There was nothing there. He turned back towards the window and modern Mexico City was back as it was supposed to be, with all the taxis and buses and pedestrians that belonged there.

He sat on the bed trying to rationalize it all. Blood dripped down onto his hand. He reached up and felt again to make sure at least that part of the morning was real and he went into the bathroom to bandage the cut. When he was finished he walked back into the room, laid down and went to sleep again.

Around 7am he found himself looking up at the ceiling. He could feel the Band-Aid. He thought about the dream and shook his head in puzzlement. He got up and decided to call the airline. Before he started to dial, he had an urge to stand up and look out the window again. He looked out and all was normal and has it should have been. He sat back down and dialed the airline. He was told the volcano warning had been lifted. His flight was cleared to leave at 6:35pm that evening. "Perfect", he thought "I can sleep for another couple of hours".

He lay down and was quickly asleep. But he dreamt again. This time it was not as graphic the late night dream. It was a dark dream; he was in a dark place. The only light was a deep purple glow from a point in the dark, he could not tell how far. He felt something rub against his legs and reached down. It was some kind of animal. He started to move away when he heard the voice calling him. It was the same voice he heard the night before. It was Iuitl. He felt the animal against him again. He yelled in panic and woke himself up. He sat up and soon there was a knock on the door. "Senor, Senor are you well? Do you need help?" He went to the door and opened it. The hotel maid stared at him looking especially concerned about the bandage on his head. He told her everything was Ok he just had a nightmare. She said that she had heard him cry out several times in the last hour and the front desk said that his neighbors had heard him late into the night. He again said that he was Ok and thanked her for her concern.

By now it was 10am. Check out time at the Nikko was 11am so he needed to dress and pack up. He was very tired but he did not want to go to sleep again. He decided that maybe he would eat and then go out for a walk to clear his head. He called the front desk and asked for a late check out at 4pm. Since he was well known at the hotel and a good tipper, the clerk said yes, he could definitely stay until 4.

153

With that out of the way he dressed and went down to eat. While he ate and thought about what had been happening to him, he decided it would be a good day to go to the Basilica De Guadalupe. It wasn't far and it was somewhere he went often when he had a few extra hours in the city. It was a good place to sit and think, very relaxing and peaceful especially if there weren't hordes of tourists or pilgrims around. He finished eating and went out and got a hotel cab.

In 1981 he had written an article about the appearance of the Virgin of Guadalupe to an Indian peasant in 1532. It supposedly happened on a hill dedicated to the Mexica Mother Goddess Tonantzin Chimalma. His article detailed the history of the descriptions and writings about the event. The conclusion was that the apparition was most likely invented by the Spanish conquerors to help pacify and covert the Indians to Catholicism. His conclusion was that even if the apparition had not really happened, this place was still holy and miraculous, if only because of the faith and belief that millions of people had for it. But his bosses had decided not to publish the article for fear of creating an unnecessary offense to millions of people in the US and Mexico.

Stephen's personal religious or spiritual beliefs did not preclude an appearance by the Virgin Mary, but in this instance he felt that even though the evidence had shown that it was faked, perhaps it did not really matter. Sometimes the myth was more important than reality. At the Basilica the usual groups of school kids, Japanese tourists and nuns were waiting to go inside and get on the moving walkway to view the tilma[31]. what is thought to be the miraculous image of Guadalupe, but there weren't many people out walking around the grounds. He decided to walk up the hill to the shrine on Tepeyac hill where tradition says that apparition occurred. He was about half way up when suddenly he looked around and there was something falling from the sky. It was volcanic ash. Popo[32] had erupted after all. He wondered if his flight would be cancelled again. He continued walking, looking around at the ash and thinking about how much it resembled snow, at least while it was falling. He made it up to the little gift and refreshment shop in front of Capilla del Cerrito[33], brushed off a bench and sat down. A priest walked by and told him that he should get inside; it wasn't healthy to breathe the ash. He told the priest that he needed to sit for a while longer. The Priest blessed him, handed him a face mask and walked off. Stephen watched the priest walk down the hill. He looked around at the Chapel, and the wooded area. He imagined the Holy Mother appearing to the Indian Juan Diego at this very

---

[31] A shawl or cloak

[32] Popo is the popular name for the largest and most active volcano near Mexico - Popocatapetl

[33] The chapel, built on the spot where Guadalupe is thought to have appeared

spot or at least very close by. Then remembered Tomas's description of the visitation at Salamanca. As he sat deep in thought, he felt something cool on his cheek and focused again at what was falling from the sky. The ash was gone and deep red rose petals were falling. He stood up with his hands out catching the petals. He remembered Tomas's description of the apparition of the Virgin on top of the temple. Tomas had said that rose petals fell from the sky. He looked up and around to see where they were coming from and suddenly they stopped and ash was falling again. He thought of all that had happened to him during the last two days and now this. He asked himself if he was going crazy. As he stood up he felt off balance, just as he had during the earthquake. He felt as if he could no longer really tell what was solid and real and what was not. He still had some of the petals in his hand. He finally threw them up in the air and walked off.

He walked back towards the hotel for a while before he finally decided to hail a cab. He hadn't even noticed when the ash stopped falling. After he got back to the hotel he sat in the bar until about 3:30. Then he went back up to his room, got his bags and left for the airport. He arrived and was soon onboard in his first class seat, waiting for the doors to close and the flight home to begin. As he took off his jacket and folded it to put up in the overhead, he could feel something in one of the pockets. He pulled it out. It was the stone from the dog's collar that he picked up before the rain storm the day before. He turned in over in his hand. He was wondering why the stone had not been spotted by security at the airport or at the Basilica. A voice from the across the aisle told him to stop shining the light in his face. He looked over at the man who did indeed have light shining in his face. Stephen said that it wasn't his light. As he said this, without thinking, he closed his fist around the stone and the light stopped. He wasn't even aware of what he had done when the man thanked him. Stephen was confused and again not quite sure what was going on. He looked around the cabin, slipped the stone back into the pocket, sat back with the jacket in his lap, and closed his eyes.

The next thing he knew was feeling the flight attendant squeezing his shoulder and telling him to wake up. He looked out the window and saw that the plane had taken off. She said that he had been having a nightmare and the noises he was making were disturbing the other passengers. He turned his head and looked at her blankly for a few seconds and said "Sorry, please bring me a rum and diet coke."

As he sat there thinking, he consumed three rums. When he ordered the fourth, the flight attendant said she would bring it to him, but after that she could not serve him anymore. It was then that he noticed his seat mate and others in the cabin furtively glancing at him with worried looks in their eyes. He took a book out of his bag and began to read trying not to make eye contact with anyone. But he would read a few sentences and involuntarily look up. After a while he thought, Great ! Along with all the other crap going on, now I'm becoming paranoid.

It was the longest and most unpleasant flight he had ever had. The plane finally landed in Portland. He gathered his bag and walked off the plane. When he got into the terminal he noticed two uniformed airport police looking at him closely and following him through customs and then out of the airport.

On the second day after he arrived home, he called his boss and editor, Jim, and said he wasn't feeling well and needed a few days off and more time to finish the article. This was the first time in nearly 17 years that he had called in sick and missed a deadline. Jim and his colleagues were all quite surprised.

On the third day, his wife, Joice, started to get worried. He had not been able to get a restful period of sleep since the day of the earthquake. Because of his nightmares and dreams, he kept Joice awake and she hadn't had much sleep either. Since he had been home the dreams were less defined. He did not remember exactly what happened but they were dark dreams of blood and death. He had tried to finish the article but every time he sat down to write, the shadow of his dreams would appear and they were all he could think of. If he sat long enough, with his eyes closed he could begin to remember scenes from the dreams. When this happened he would open his eyes and a shiver would run through his body.

He started to drink a lot more than usual. When he got drunk he could get a little sleep, but even then only for short periods. On the fifth day Jim called Joice and wanted to know what was wrong. He said that Stephen had called and asked for more time off and he sounded like he was drunk. Joice answered that she was very worried. Perhaps he had acquired some kind of disease in Mexico. She told Jim that she would take Stephen to the doctor the next day.

The doctor told them that Stephen was most likely suffering from some sort of hallucinogenic symptoms of exhaustion. He gave him some anti-anxiety medication to help him sleep. He told Stephen that if he did not feel better in five days he would need to see a psychologist and maybe get a brain MRI.

Five days went by and the medication was helping. The dreams still came, but not as often. He was sleeping more and he had been able to cut back on his drinking. Before starting the medication, during the rare times when he was sober, he had started to catalog and describe the dreams, There were two kinds of dreams; graphic dreams of events (bloody events) happening in a Pre-Hispanic Mexican city. He thought it was Tenochtitlan, but of course he couldn't be sure; the other type was more difficult it was a surreal dream usually in a dark place and usually with odd, menacing humanoid/hybrid creatures. The one thing that seemed to connect all the dreams was Iuitl's voice and occasional glimpses of someone that might have been her.

Because he was getting more sleep, he went back to work. But when he was working, he would doze off at his desk and dream two or more times per day. When this happened he would talk in his sleep, he would yell and curse or appear to be very frightened. One of these episodes happened at a very bad time. He was meeting with Richard, a regional manager and his boss's boss. Richard arrived, Stephen shook his hand and as they walked to the conference room they exchanged the usual small talk about sports and family. When they got down to business Richard began explaining an idea for a story. As Richard talked and diagramed his thoughts on the white board, Stephen nodded off and began to dream talk and shake and gesture wildly. Richard stopped talking, looked curiously at him and tried to wake him. Finally he walked out of the room, leaving Stephen asleep, and very disoriented when he awoke a few minutes later.

Richard went directly to Jim's office and barged in without knocking and demanded to know what was going on. "Is Stephen on some kind of drugs?" he asked. Jim was well aware of what was going on and apologized to Richard saying that Stephen had been working too hard and had a nervous breakdown after his last trip to Mexico. Jim said that Stephen was on a medication and was doing better, but he was not back to his normal self yet. Jim promised to get in touch with Joice and make sure Stephen got back to the doctor right away. Richard shook his head and said that everyone needed to pull their weight and be productive; Stephen had already caused problems by missing a deadline and not finishing the article. Jim said he agreed and understood, they shook hands and Richard left.

Jim watched Richard walk down the hall and then went over to the conference room. Stephen had just awakened and sat there with his face in his hands. Jim said, "Look Steve, we can't go on like this. You need to get back to the doctor and get whatever is going on with you fixed. If you want an early retirement we can do it. But you can't come back to the office and work until you can stay awake." Without saying anything, Stephen got up and left.

The dreams and the lack of sleep were ruining his life, both at work and at home. The suspicious part of his brain began to think that there must be some connection to Martin,

Maurilio and Iuitl. He was thinking maybe they gave him some kind of long lasting hallucinogen or something. The connection to them and his problems was just too strong

He decided that he had to go back to Mexico City and Calle Mina and start asking questions. He needed to see Iuitl again and find out why she was showing up in all his dreams. He had only met her once on that one day a few weeks before. He had thought that she was interesting and he was curious about her. But he didn't think that she had made such an impression on his brain that he would constantly hear her calling him in his dreams.

Joice was almost violently opposed to him going back to back. She yelled, she cried, she called his doctor. Stephen listened to her, tried to convince her that he had to find out what was going on. She started to yell again and told him that if he left he should not come back. He walked outside, got into the car and drove to the airport. He bought a ticket and stayed the night at an airport hotel

Early the next morning he was on a plane on his way to Mexico. Before he boarded he took two of the anti-anxiety pills and hoped they would keep him out of trouble during the flight.

He only fell asleep once or twice on the plane and nobody said anything to him, so he assumed that he had not dream talked or done anything to scare or annoy the other passengers. After the plane landed, he went through customs with no problem and walked outside to get an airport taxi. His first stop was the hotel to drop off his luggage. Usually when he arrived in the City he enjoyed relaxing in the taxi and looking at all the shops and houses and bill boards as they passed, but today in the deep background of his mind, Iuitl's voice kept calling him. In a closer more conscience part of his brain all the questions he wanted to ask Martin and Maurilio made an endless loop. When he arrived at the hotel, he paid and tipped the driver and asked him to wait. He got out of the taxi and was greeted by the attendant in the driveway with usual courtesy and cheerfulness that Mexicans show to guests. He told the attendant his name and said he would check in later. He asked if they would hold his bags. He said he was late for an appointment. The attendant remembered his name from previous visits. He quickly scribbled a receipt and as he handed it to Stephen, he said "Very well Senor Saldivar, we will see you later".

Stephen got back into the cab and told the driver to go to Calle Mina, near the Cathedral. The driver looked back at him like he thought maybe he had misunderstood. He said," Senor, are you sure. Calle Mina is not a place where people from your country usually go, the buildings are old and it may not be a safe place for a man like you." "I know what's there", Stephen told him," I have been there before. I am going to visit my cousins". The driver turned again, looked intensely at him for a moment and then said "Si Senor, Calle Mina."

They drove past the park and turned on to Avenida de la Reforma. It was a very sunny and clear day in the City. The normal brown gray smog had blown away. He could actually see the mountains in the distance. As they drove by the giant Angel of Independence statue he noticed that the gold plating was brighter and shinier then he had ever seen it. He supposed that it must have recently been cleaned. Soon they drove past the Cathedral and the Zocolo and in a few minutes they were on the corner of Calle Mina and Calle Argentina. The cab stopped. The driver asked if he should wait. Stephen paid and thanked him and said that he could go. He gave Stephen his card and said to call when he was done.

The street and the buildings did not have the same surreal feeling now than they did the last time he visited. The sun and clear air made the cobblestone street and buildings look straighter and almost normal. He walked down the street a short distance and found what he thought was the doorway he had entered to get out of the rain last month. He knocked and there was no answer. He was not quite sure about the etiquette of a building like this. He remembered that this outer door opened to a courtyard with inner doors leading to the interior dwellings. He decided to open the outer door and go in. There were six more doors arranged around a courtyard. He was not sure which of these doors was the one he wanted. As he stood there looking and trying to remember, one of the doors opened. A young man dressed in an old business suit about two sizes too big walked out and looked over at him and spoke to him in Spanish. "If you are the bill collector, go away, we have no money and no one is here but me. As you can see I'm looking for the job now. Come back next week." Stephen's Spanish was good enough to understand most of what the young man said. He answered. "I am not a bill collector; I am looking for Martin and Maurilio Saldivar. They are my cousins. Could you tell me which door is theirs?" The young man looked surprised and said in English, "you have old accent, you are of states? I go states soon, maybe Texas. I get good job. Her is door you need" He pointed to one of the doors. Stephen thanked him, praised his English, wished him good luck, turned and knocked on the door that the young man had pointed to.

Soon he could hear someone coming to the door. A voice spoke from behind the door telling Stephen to go away. Stephen said "Maurilio, is that you? I am sorry to bother you again. Do you remember me? I am Esteban Saldivar, I need to talk to you, I am having dreams, strange and intense dreams that seem to be related to Iuitl and the book you loaned me a few weeks ago." There was a shuffling, and behind the door he could hear latches and locks being undone. The door opened and Maurilio stood inside looking disheveled and very tired and old. "Come in Esteban", he said. "We are glad you came. I dream also and the dreams have come once more now that Iuitl has left us again." Stephen could see Martin coming down the hall. As Martin walked in he began to speak, "Maurilio, Close the door. Esteban, it is good to see you again, please sit down. Are you well? Did you read Tomas's book? Can I get you something to drink?" Stephen sat down at the table, declined the offer of a drink. The two brothers also sat down and they exchanged the usual pleasantries. Stephen asked, "Yes I read the book, it ended very abruptly". Maurilio answered, "Yes, the conquest of the city ended a lot of things very abruptly. But what did you think of Tomas and all he had to say about the Mexica, the conquest and the appearance of the Virgin?" Stephen shook his head, looked down for a moment and then back up at Maurilio," I'm not sure the book is authentic. I've read all the historical evidence and firsthand accounts of the conquest and there were no hints of any of the religious unrest that Tomas says was happening. The whole story seems like a work of fiction, in some parts almost fantasy, but not a real history." Maurilio nodded and laughed a little. "Esteban, you are an intelligent man. You read a lot of history? If so, then I am sure you understand that history, especially history of conquest and conflict, is written by the victors. They want to justify what they did. The Conquistadors in Mexico were greedy, cruel men. They wanted gold and land and slaves. The only reason they wanted to convert the native people to Christianity was to help control them and make them docile slaves. They were not missionaries Esteban. But there is one little historical reference that they tried to eliminate and perhaps were not completely successful. Do you remember the name Ocelotl? This was the Indian disciple that Tomas mentioned at least twice. Father Esteban also mentions an Indian named Martin Ocelotl. He is an historical figure. Many of the accounts of the period after the conquest mention Ocelotl. They called him a sorcerer and eventually a heretic. He was a man who had a very large following among the Indians, practicing what the conquerors called demon worship. But remember Father Esteban called him a Christian Indian. He said that Ocelotl claimed to be a witness to the appearance of the Holy Mother. In 1536, not long after he found the book and gave it to Father Esteban, Ocelotl was tried and convicted by the inquisition. In those days most Indians convicted by the inquisition were burned alive the day they were judged. But Ocelotl was sent to Spain and he died in a church prison. I have tried to find an explanation for this but I cannot. The fact that Tomas mentions Ocelotl as a disciple and the fact that the Inquisition sent him to Spain to be questioned by the highest of the learned fathers appears to be evidence of some historical connection to a religious controversy and possibly Tomas.

Esteban, listen to me, the reason that Tomas's manuscript is so important is that it reveals that the Mesoamerican culture was about to make a big shift away from all the bloody gods. They were ready to give up human sacrifice and begin to worship one god. Let me try to explain what I think was happening. There was a Chinese Emperor in the 6th century, he said something very profound. Let me think". He paused for a moment and then said, "This is it, close at least, you will understand,

"The way has not, at all times and places, the selfsame name; the sage has not, at all times and places, the selfsame body. Heaven caused a suitable religion to be instituted for every region and clime so that each one of the races of mankind might be saved. "

You see Esteban, cultures evolve just as organisms do. God reveals itself to different cultures in different ways. The problem is that the European culture has violently pushed its calcified version of God off onto the rest of the world." Martin touched Maurilio's shoulder. "That's enough, Maurilio. You and Esteban can discuss history and theology later. Esteban is saying that he has been having troubling dreams. You know better than anyone that we need to talk about that now."

Maurilio looked at Stephen and said, "Yes, tell us about your dreams, tell us what the dreams are about? What are they telling you?" Stephen started to answer, but suddenly remembered what Maurilio had said about Iuitl. "What's happened to Iuitl? Where has she gone?" he asked. "She's gone. We don't really know where" said Martin. "Have you seen her in your dreams?" He told them "Yes, I think so, but how did you know? It is very unnerving and a little frightening. I dream every night, sometime I just fall into a dream in the day. I am dreaming of the Mexica and their grotesque gods over and over again. Do you know why this is happening to me?" The brothers looked at each other. Maurilio stood up and went into the back. He returned with a fragment of smooth black obsidian. "Have you ever seen anything like this?" "Yes" said Stephen," A piece like that dropped off a dog's collar right out in front of your building on the day we first met. I picked it up and put it in my pocket". The bothers looked at each other. "Well that explains part of it at least. We really don't know why all this is happening to you. Maybe it is an accident. Iuitl can explain it all when she returns" said Martin. "But before we talk about your dreams, let Maurilio tell you about his life and his dreams."

Part 4 Maurilio and Martin

Maurilio looked at Martin and said, "By now you know it as well as I do, you tell the story. I'm tired". Maurilio got up, nodded at Stephen, turned and walked down the hall. Martin watched him walk away and then began the story.

"As you know, Maurilio and I are brothers. Our family was not rich, but neither were we poor. Our father was a rope maker and a surveyor. We lived in a modest house in Jerez, Zacatecas. Tomas's book and the codex were family possessions. My father and his fathers could not read the manuscript and did not know much about it except they thought that it was written by one of our ancestors who been with Cortez during the conquest. We kept it as an heirloom. It was a curiosity that was one of those things that is always just there. We all just took it for granted. As far as I can remember we really never discussed it and rarely took it off the shelf to look at it. And as far as the codex goes, well, there was a family tradition that made it clear that if anyone unrolled, it would be a sin that would release devils.

Maurilio was the oldest child. There were two sisters and myself. I was the youngest. Our father wanted Maurilio to be a surveyor. But Maurilio loved to read histories and wanted to go to the National University in Mexico City to become an historian or a teacher. Our father was against it, but mother convinced him. She said that a historian can write books and become famous and make a lot of money. Father reluctantly agreed and in 1912, Maurilio left for the university. This was a difficult time in Mexico. The fighting that would soon become the revolution had started.

I was very young and cannot remember Maurilio. But I do remember through the years our family talking about him and wondering what had happened to him. I was told that we got regular letters from him for a few years or so. But when the letters stopped we knew nothing of his life until 1932 when he returned home and I finally met him. It was then that he told the story of his life in the twenty or so years since he left home.

During his first year at the university he took a job as a digger at a construction site very close to where we are now, here on Calle Mina. The fighting in the north did not affect him. There were plenty of Indians and peons for the army so university students were not bothered much.

One day while his construction crew was digging, they began to uncover remnants of a Mexica structure. In those days it was common to find these remnants, mostly ignore them, and continue the work. But being a history student Maurilio was fascinated by some of the things he found. The construction foreman knew the pottery, the carvings and other things were valuable so he usually kept what the diggers found.

One day Maurilio uncovered some flat glassy black stones. They were very dirty and scratched but they reflected light. If he wiped and cleaned them a little he could almost see a shadow of his reflection. He put several of them in his pocket and did not tell the supervisor he had found them. He hid all but one of the stones under the floor boards in the apartment where he was living. The one he kept was small. It appeared to be a piece that had broken off one of the larger stones. He kept this fragment in his pocket as a good luck charm.

A few months after he found the stones, the revolution came to Mexico City, Francisco Madero, our first democratically elected President in almost 50 years, was jailed and executed. General Victoriano Huerta became president. Maurilio, like many young people, had been a supporter of Madero. Huerta began to draft young men into the army. Maurilio was one of them. He considered running away to join one of the anti Huerta armies in the north, but there were guards around the camp where he had been taken and he knew he would be shot if he tried to escape. He was given a rifle, a uniform and very little training and sent to the north to fight.

Maurilio was nearly killed in the battle for Zacatecas. He was left to die, bleeding in the battlefield. He managed to crawl to a shelter where he was nursed by a teenage girl, Seraphina, and her brother. They had come from a rancho in the countryside hoping to get on a train and go to the USA. Of course the battle delayed all trains except those carrying soldiers. But Huerta's army had been defeated. Pancho Villa and the Army of the North headed south towards the capital. Soon the trains began to arrive again.

After a few weeks, the Seraphina, her brother and Maurilio climbed on to the roof of one of the trains. They spent six days on top of the train, only getting off to find water or food when the train stopped. In those days there were many people escaping Mexico and the fighting. The tops of the trains were crowded. It was a difficult trip but mostly people were kind to each other. They all had the same goal.

When Maurilio and his friends reached Arizona, they found there was no work. They heard stories and rumors that there was a lot of work in California. The orchards and farms needed labor. With Mexico in chaos, the USA was looking to California to grow the crops that previously had come from across the border. California was booming. The Seraphina's brother had a little money and was able to get bus tickets for the three of them to go to Los Angeles.

When they arrived they met a group at the bus station who told them they were going about 40 miles north to work for a new fruit growing and packing company called Lemonaria. Maurilio, the Seraphina and her brother got on another bus and within a few days they all had jobs.

Three years later, Maurilio married the Seraphina. The Lemonaria Company built a little village for the workers to live. Because Maurilio had been to the university, the others workers respected him and he became a leader of their little community. Seraphina and Maurilio had three children over the next five years. It was a happy life for them until one day Maurilio started dreaming. These dreams were like yours Esteban. Of course when you dream you must be asleep, but the sleep of a dreamer is not a sleep of rest as I think you know.

All through his time in the army and in California, Maurilio had managed to keep one of the little stones he found in Mexico City. He kept it as a good luck charm. At night he set it on the window sill next to his bed.

The dreams became steadily more vivid and more frightening. Maurilio told Seraphina that the stone actually glowed at night. She said she thought it just reflected the lights outside the window."

At this point Stephen interrupted Martin. "That's like the stone I found, a small polished, smooth faced, black obsidian stone that also seems to glow."

Martin nodded and said, "Let me finish the story and I will tell you what your stone is and why it is might be connected to your dreams.

After several months of dreaming and not really sleeping, Maurilio was becoming increasingly tired. His lack of restful sleep made him quarrelsome. He also started to drink, hoping that if he drank enough the dreams would disappear and he could sleep soundly. His work was suffering. During the day he would sit down to rest and drift off in a dream. Seraphina and his friends were becoming worried about him. They tried to hide what was happening from the bosses. Seraphina worked hard to care for the children and to help finish Maurilio's work.

There was a small bar on the side of a hill near Lemonaria. In the evenings Maurilio would go there and drink. He could see the ocean from the window of the bar. He would drink, and stare out a window looking out to the ocean. He would "see" things as he looked out the window. He became a curiosity to the Anglos at the bar. They paid for his drinks and laughed at him when he told them what he saw. It was always a shining white city he saw in the ocean. He

described the high pyramids and glimmering canals in detail.
They all laughed at him and called him a crazy Mexican.
The other Mexicans just sat there stone faced. They hoped
that Maurilio would stop talking and go home.

One night, while sitting in the bar, he cried out that the city
was burning. He screamed that he had to help and he ran
outside yelling and started down the dirt road towards the
ocean. The Anglos in the bar roared with laughter. Some of
the Mexicans ran after him and tried to stop him. He was
very drunk and easy to catch, but he fought hard and would
not stop yelling and fighting. Soon an Anglo policeman came.
Maurilio tried to fight the policeman who eventually clubbed
him, handcuffed him and took him away.

The next day Seraphina and the foreman from Lemonaria
arrived at the jail to take Maurilio home. He was calmer but
still delusional. You must remember, real restful sleep had
eluded him for almost a year. He was now in a semi dream
state all the time. He walked through the orchards and
houses at all hours, talking to himself. Somedays they found
him lying deathlike under a lemon tree."

Stephen shook his head, interrupted Martin and said "all
this is the same thing that's been happening to me."

Martin nodded, "That is what I was afraid of when you mentioned dreams. I am sorry Stephen, but let me continue and perhaps you will understand more."

"Maurilio and Seraphina's children were teased by other children. Gossip in the small company village was a popular recreational activity, especially among the women. Maurilio and Seraphina became the subject of much of this talk.

After a few months of this the bosses came to Seraphina and said that they were sorry but Maurilio could no longer work and the family would need to move. Seraphina had known this would eventually happen. She told the bosses that she was sending Maurilio back to Mexico to recuperate. She had an old letter from his family and she knew where they lived, at least where they had lived 12 years before. She said she would stay and work and as the children grew they could work also. The bosses talked among themselves and finally agreed that Seraphina and the children could stay but Maurilio must go.

Seraphina sat with Maurilio and told him that her patience with him had reached the breaking point. She was convinced that he had become a drunkard. She said that her life and their children's lives would be easier without him. So she wrote a letter to his family and mailed it the next day. Three days after mailing the letter she heard that one of the companeros at Lemonaria, a man named Leon, was planning to go back to Mexico to care for his ailing mother. Sarafina gave Leon some money and bought Maurilio a ticket for the same bus Leon was traveling on. She asked the Leon to take care of Maurilio and make sure he got off the bus in Jerez.

It was a long hot ride on several buses. First they went to Los Angeles, Then to Yuma and from there they walked across the border, where they got a bus in Los Algodones and headed south east through Mexico. There were several stops and changes in Mexico. But eventually, almost 8 days after leaving Lemonaria, they arrived in Zacatecas City. It was there that Leon left him. By this time Maurilio thought he had regained his sanity. He had slept on the long days in the bus and his dreams diminished. He says that he lost the color and clarity of the earlier dreams and they were harder to remember.

It had been nearly 20 years since he left Jerez, he hoped that we were still in the house he had known and he hoped we would remember him. It is about 50 kilometers from Zacatecas to Jerez. Not a difficult walk but the land is hard and dry. Maurilio had no money. Leon had taken what was left of the money that Seraphina had given him. He hitched a ride on a cattle truck and arrived in Jerez about late at night. He walked down the streets of the city past the Edificio de Torre, the beautiful girl's school where our sisters had been educated. When he came to our house, we were all asleep. Our father had died three years before, one of our sisters had died in the revolution and I was left with my mother and an older sister. I was about 14 years old at the time. It was 1932 and even though the revolution had been over for about 12 years, there was still civil unrest and fighting in some places because of the conflict between the church and the government.

Maurilio knocked at the door. I was reluctant to open it at such a late hour.. But I got up, as did my sister, and we went to the door. I yelled at the closed door, "Who are you, what do you want?" "I am Maurilio Saldivar, my family lived here years ago, I am looking for them" was the answer. My sister screamed, she was old enough to remember Maurilio. Our mother was awakened by the noise and as I opened the door she came stumbling down the hall.

Our family reunion was loud and tearful. My mother and sister led Maurilio into the kitchen and began to cook for him, all the while talking and asking question about his children and family and thanking God that he was safe and they could be with him again.

Over the next few weeks Maurilio and I got to know each other. He told us all about his dreams and his breakdown. My mother was convinced that it was easy for devils to invade the soul of a man when he was in the north. It was a godless place she said.

Soon Maurilio began to think about returning to California and his family. He wrote letters to Seraphina to tell her that he was cured, he had stopped drinking, he was sleeping and the dreams had stopped. He received only one letter back from her. It said that the children were healthy and happy and she was busy with work. She said that it was best if he did not return. During the next year he sent many letters begging her to allow him back.

After repeatedly reading Seraphina's letter, Maurilio became melancholy. He got a job and worked regularly. But when he was home he just sat and worried. I tried to talk to him about his life, about the revolution and about the USA. He rarely responded with much besides one word answers.

Our mother worried about him. She yearned to see and get to know his children. She occasionally berated him for not going back and bringing Seraphina and the children to our home. She would tell us that nothing good would come of them living in such an ungodly country with no father to guide them. In the next few years photographs of the children would appear. Our mother had begun a correspondence with Seraphina and she sent photos and reports on their lives in California.

One day, in an effort to have a conversation with Maurilio, I picked up Tomas's book. It had always fascinated me. When our father was alive, he occasionally referred to it and showed it to us but always made it known that we were not to touch it. I decided that since Maurilio was our family's oldest son perhaps he knew more about it. I took it down from its place and handed it to him. I told him what I remembered father saying about it and asked if he knew anything more. We were both a little afraid of the codex and left it in its place.

He told me that late at night or on days when father was working, he would take the book from the shelf and carefully page through it. He could not read much of it, only a few words here and there, but he said that just looking at the ornate lettering and smelling the ancient cover and pages gave him much pleasure. He would sit with it in his hands and day dream of the Mexica and the famous conquistadors. He then sighed and said that those day dreams had become the nightmares that had ruined his life in California.

After I handed it to him, he looked down at it and said that he was not sure he should open it again. He continued looked at it and then at me and then down at the book again. He sat down and after a moment of hesitation, he opened it.

181

In the next few days, Maurilio became obsessed with the book. He would spend hours on just one page trying to decipher the calligraphy and translate the archaic words. At first he kept notes on a tablet. As the weeks went by his notes were becoming a full translation. In the evenings when we ate, he would sit at the table and read pages of the book to us. Our sister and mother were never very interested, but I always listened eagerly. Soon I was helping him. I would go to book stalls in the markets of Zacatecas and look for old dictionaries and histories that might help him understand what he was reading. We worked out time lines and dates. Tomas's handwriting and the ink he used changed in the final pages. The letters became less ornate and the spacing more irregular. We found that he occasionally even left out words. Some pages were completely missing. The spelling also deteriorated. We began a catalog of his handwriting, so we could compare the changes. This helped us quite a bit. The final pages were very difficult.

Towards the end of the book, while working on his translation, Maurilio talked to himself quite a bit. Listening to him as he talked worried me somewhat, the things he said seemed to indicate that he knew what was going to happen next and that he recognized certain people and places. Sometimes he would look up from the book and his typewriter, stroke his mustache and stare out the window for several minutes and then smiling and nodding he would continue his work.

One day I finally asked him about this behavior. He looked at me closely and said that I might think he was crazy, but he had seen the places and people and events described in the book several years before in the dreams that brought about his breakdown. He said that he was a little frightened by this but it was almost like seeing old friends again. He made it clear to me that when the translation was completed he would work to discover why his dreams and the book seemed to be connected in his mind.

Maurilio had started reading and making notes in March 1935. When we finished the first draft translation in September 1937, he decided that we should start from the beginning again and using the knowledge we had gained during the first reading, and from the memories of his dreams, we should go back and make sure the context and actual translations were correct. Finally in August 1938, Maurilio was satisfied that we had truly and correctly translated Tomas's Autobiography. I was a little worried that perhaps his dreams might have influenced the translation. Perhaps the translation was more fictional than factual. But even so I felt the book was a very interesting story of a very unusual man.

After finishing the translation from archaic handwritten Spanish calligraphy to modern Spanish, Maurilio decided to make another translation from Spanish to English. This, he said, was for his children back in California.

This next task was easy compared to the first translation. I was learning English, Maurilio was nearly fluent and there was a man we knew, an American from Connecticut, who lived in Jerez. The American, his name was Harry Witt, was a writer. He helped immensely with our grammar, our word choice, our punctuation and all the other skills and knowledge in English writing that we lacked.

In only four months we completed the English version. Harry told us that he knew a publisher and that he thought perhaps we should send the manuscript to America for evaluation. This required us to make a copy. As you know, Esteban, in those days there were no copy machines. It all needed to be hand typed again. So we retyped the English version and sent it to the address that Harry had given us. We never heard anything from the USA and we pretty much forgot about the English translation until 1948 when our sister Vera forwarded a letter from a publisher. He said that there was a bestselling novel that had a very similar theme. "Captain from Castile" was its name. It had recently become a Technicolor movie. He said he would publish the book and try to capitalize on the movie's success. He did not pay us but enclosed a contract that promised 10% royalty on sales and said he would send us a few copies that we could try to sell in Mexico. But I am rambling off the point of the story. Let me return to the events of 1938 and 9.

After the English translation was finished and mailed, we decided that we needed to take the original book and the translation to the university in the capital.

I was concerned about leaving our mother and our sister Vera. When we announced our plans, Vera told us not to worry, she said, "I can take care of mother, we have enough money to live comfortably, so go publish your book and become famous". So with tearful goodbyes, we set out for the capital.

The only real city I had ever experienced was Zacatecas. I was not prepared for the size and complexity of Mexico City. Even then, in 1939, it was busy and crowded. We found and rented these rooms on Calle Mina on the first day we were in the city. We have lived here ever since.

After getting settled, we took the manuscript and translation to Professor Lucas Aleman at the University. He was a specialist and expert in letters and books written by the conquistadors. We learned about his work while doing the research for the translation.

He spent about 30 minutes paging through the manuscript and comparing it with the translation. Finally he said that he wanted us to leave the manuscript with him. He congratulated us on our work. But be indicated, politely of course, that Maurilio did not have the education or background to do an accurate translation. As I said he was polite, but the message he gave was that Maurilio's translation was trash and that we needed to give him the manuscript so that he could authenticate it and make a serious translation. Maurilio was insulted. We picked up the manuscript, walked out and never returned.

Maurilio sat and stewed for about a month. He didn't know what to do until we met Lucinda.

In the mornings we would go to a small coffee shop near San Illdefonso. Lucinda was also a patron of this shop. One day Maurilio and I were talking about the book and discussing what we should do next. Lucinda overheard us. She leaned over from her table and told us that she was embarrassed that she had been listening to our conversation, but that she might be able to help us. I could tell from his expression that Maurilio was suspicious. But we invited her over to sit with us. She asked us to tell her what kind of book we had. We told her the whole story, leaving out Maurilio's dreams and breakdown. She told us that we had been wise not to leave it with Dr. Aleman. "You would have never seen it again", she said, "except maybe in a Museum". We learned that she studied Literature at the university and she worked at a large used bookstore. She dressed and spoke like one of the young intellectuals of the day. Nowadays we would say that she was "cool and hip". In her social circle were many of the writers and poets in the city.

She told us we needed to get certificate of ownership for the original book and then a copy-write for the translation. We both wondered about how we could get a certificate of ownership. The book had been in our family for 500 years and no one that we knew of had ever seen it but our family. "That makes it difficult", she said, "Perhaps it would be better to give it to the University". Maurilio was almost violently opposed to this. I told him to calm down and perhaps we needed to return home and talk to our mother and other older relatives. Perhaps one of them would know something that would help us. Lucinda listened and then offered an idea. She said that maybe we should publish the translation first and then if there was interest and questions from scholars and historians, we could unveil the manuscript and our story of ownership. Maurilio frowned, furrowed his brow and narrowed his eyes as he does when he is seriously thinking about a new idea. He sat like that for a few minutes and then looked up and said that he thought we should try Lucinda's plan. She smiled and said that she knew some small publishers in the city, but it might be expensive.

A few days later she took us to meet a man who owned a small print shop and bindery. He was very fat and he chain smoked. I thought to myself that perhaps all his books would smell like stale cigarettes. We gave him a synopsis of the story and he said we should leave the translation and he would read it and make a decision in the next few weeks.

We went back to see him after 9 days. He said that the story was sound. He was worried about the ending. "The ending just, well, it just ends. There is no climax for the story. It needs a better ending. Also it needs more drama and more love interest." We laughed at this and again told him that it was a translation of an ancient manuscript. He shook his head and said "Listen my friends, I am a professional, I get ten or twenty of these historical romances per year. All of the authors, of course, claim they are true." Lucinda told him that she had seen the manuscript and it certainly appeared to be authentic. "Well, regardless, here are your options. If you allow me to edit it and you make the changes I suggest, I can print, bind and distribute 50 copies for 50 pesos per copy plus a sales commission of 15%. If you insist on printing it as is, I will not distribute it and there would be no commission, and the price would be 90 pesos per copy for 50 copies." The exchange rate then was roughly 5 pesos to one

US dollar, so as you can see Esteban, in 1939 this was a very expensive proposition. We had some money to live on and pay our rent, but we could not afford this.

We decided to get jobs and save our money for a few months and then try again perhaps with another publisher.

One morning, about three weeks later, as we sat and drank our coffee, Lucinda told us about a very odd customer whom she thought we should meet. "It was early" she began," A small Indian woman, came into the store. The owner of the store, Senor Guzman is a bigot. When people like this come in to the store he thinks they are beggars who come in to beg from our customers or steal something from the store. He tried to lead the Indian woman out. She spoke a very formal and old fashioned Spanish. She seemed to be a well-educated woman. She told us she was looking for firsthand accounts of the Conquest and the apparition of Guadalupe. She took a stack of pesos from her sash and said she had more. Senor Guzman, although a bigot, likes money. But he was still reluctant to have our regular customers see her in the store. He took her to a back room where there was a table and chair and asked me to bring her some books to examine. I went off to the history section and found the Letters of Cortez, the books by Bernal Diaz, Las Casas, Sahagun and several books about Our Lady of Guadalupe. I brought them to her. She looked at each and told me that

189

she had already read them. She asked if there was anything else. It was then that I thought of your manuscript and translation. I told her about it and she seemed very excited. I said that we met for coffee three times per week outside the College of San Illdefonso. I told her I would talk to you and we might arrange for a meeting. "Come back tomorrow", I suggested to her. "Do you want to meet her?" "Why not", Maurilio said. I agreed.

So the next morning we met Iuitl. She was dressed and looked as if she had just come out of one of the remote Indians ejidos or ranchos as they are called in English. But there was a brightness about her and she had a single red rose tucked into her hair. That was in 1939. Believe it or not Esteban, she looked the same as she does now. Since that first meeting she has lived here with us. She leaves and is gone sometimes for years but she always comes back and as I said, believe it or not, her appearance has never changed." With his arms open and hands spread out, Martin raised his eye brows and shrugged.

Stephen interrupted at this point, "This is very interesting Martin, but I need to know why I have been having these dreams. Oh and I really cannot believe that after 50 years Iuitl has not changed. I doubt that she is even 50 years old to begin with".

Martin answered, "You wanted to know about your dreams and I understand that I have not told you what you came for yet. But please be patient and soon you will understand a little more about the mystery of what has happened to you. Let me continue."

Part 5 Iuitl

"The morning we met Iuitl for the first time, she arrived at the coffee shop exactly at the appointed hour. She sat down; there was no small talk or introductions. She asked us about the book and was quite excited when we told her about it. She wanted to see it immediately. We agreed and left the coffee shop and walked the few blocks to our rooms. She did not speak until we arrived. We opened the door and she abruptly turned and asked where we were from. When we told her, Jerez in Zacatecas, she pulled out her money. It was over ten thousand pesos. She handed to us and said she would buy the book now. Maurilio let her know that the book was not for sale. He said that we were trying to publish a translation and when we raised the money he would sell her a copy. She said she did not want a translation, she said that she needed to read the original immediately. We were somewhat taken aback by her insistence.

We sat there and looked at each other for a few seconds without speaking. She cleared her throat, looked around at us and said", "You want money to publish the translation? I will pay for the publication if only I can read the original and have access to it as I need it. You see I am researching a very important historical event that may change many of our ideas about the conquest and post conquest periods."

"We were surprised by this and thought that perhaps her research may be related to Tomas. It did not take much thought for us to agree with this offer. We offered her a bottle of water and told her to sit. I went to get the book and without another word from her she handed us the money and sat down at the table where I had placed the book. She began to read very slowly. As she read it, I was reminded of Maurilio's first reading. She talked to herself as she read. Sometimes it was as if she was conversing with someone. She would stare at the wall, nodding and speaking as if someone was there. All this was in an Indian language we could not understand.

Maurilio and I went into one of the other rooms. I told Maurilio that I thought she was quite crazy. He looked at me very seriously and asked if I had noticed the black stones on her sash. I told him yes I had noticed them and I thought that they seemed to reflect light in a very unusual manner. Maurilio said, "When I was at the university I found stones like that while digging through some ruins when I was working at a construction job. I kept one with me for many years. They were some kind of obsidian fragments. I need to ask her about the ones that she wears." He went back to the room where she was reading. He told her that many years ago he had found some stones like the ones on her sash and he was interested in where she got them and what she thought they were.

This question seemed to startle her. She turned and looked hard at Maurilio while reaching and fidgeting with the stones on her sash." "They are pieces of something that was broken long ago. Where are the pieces you found?" He answered, "There were quite a few that I found, some were larger than those of yours, and some were sharp and jagged. I left them here in the City before the revolution. I kept one piece for many years. But I don't know where it is, I must have left it in California. "

"You have the book, you had pieces of a mirror, have you ever dreamed of the conquest?" she asked him. Then it was Maurilio's turn to be surprised. He sat down beside her. They just sat there and talked for several hours.

Several days after this and after she finished reading the manuscript for the first time, she took off her sash and handed it to Maurilio. She asked him to touch the stones. One of them glowed brightly, and she removed that stone and gave it to him, telling him to always keep it near.

It was then that I remembered the codex. I told her that we also had one. We were afraid of it and never unrolled it to see what it was. This excited her even more. She said that there were no devils in it and that it belonged to the manuscript. It was an illustration and the Mexica confirmation of the appearance of the Holy Mother. She said that she must see it. I told her that I wanted to visit my mother, so I would go back to Jerez and bring it to her. She gave me money for bus fare and I went to get it. I was gone nearly a month. When I returned she opened it and read the glyphs and told us that we must keep it safe until the final confirmation was made.

Now, Esteban, I think you are beginning to see that your dreams are not unique. Maurilio has had very similar experiences. His dreams were very much like yours. It seems that these pieces of black stone are fragments of the obsidian mirrors that were so important in the mythologies of all the native cultures of Mexico and Central America. They were supposed to be portals to glimpse the past and future.

And as for Iuitl, well my friend I must ask your indulgence. I can explain to you what she told us, but I do not understand it. Essentially she told us that when she is here with us, she is dreaming. She lives in the 16th century." Stephen interrupted and said, "I'm a real person, I have a real life that exists when she's not around. For god's sake I only met her once. How could I be a character in her dreams?" Martin answered "Let me explain. She says that she believes that time does not really exist as we know it. She believes that all of us, all the people who have ever lived and will ever live are only part of what exists. There are other beings who live outside of time. Time is merely a construct that our

195

minds have created to allow us to experience our life. She says that when we dream, our unconscious mind is "seeing" jumbled images of people and things happening in this timeless state. Our brain tries to put all the jumbled images together in a time reference. That process creates a dream. This is why dreams are irrational and random. The mirrors give her, Maurilio, and now maybe you, a tool to focus on specific events or people. She says the focus of her dream is to find out what happened to Tomas and to document the real appearance of the Holy Mother. She helped Maurilio understand that if one does not learn to control the mirror, insanity may follow."

Stephen sat there, scratching his head with his lips pursed and then said, "The REAL appearance of the Virgin Mary? You mean the part in Tomas's book. I had the feeling that he might have been hallucinating. Or do you mean Guadalupe, the appearance of Guadalupe at Tepepac?" "Listen", said Martin, "Iuitl told us she was present when the Virgin appeared in 1522 during the period when the Spanish were in Tenochtitlan." Stephen was obviously flustered by all this. "You're talking nonsense Martin. These are some of the craziest thing I've ever heard. They make no sense at all."

"Yes, I know. But the reality, or perhaps I should say mystery, of what we see is that Iuitl looks the same as she did 50 years ago. And of course, first Maurilio and now you have had unsettling dreams of events related to a manuscript that was written nearly 500 years ago."

Stephen did not know what to say. He sat there at the table feeling very uncomfortable. "Maybe I will have a drink" he said, "but not the Pulque. Do you have anything else?" Martin answered with a shrug," Yes we have Bohemia beer, but it's too bad because the Pulque will help you understand all this." Martin went down the hall and returned with a beer, a glass of Pulque for himself and a bag of Chicharrones for them to share.

"Now let me briefly finish the story. You are tired. I promise to minimize the mysterious things and let your brain rest.

As I have said, Iuitl came and went over the years. She would be gone for a few years or sometimes only a month or so, and then all of a sudden she would show up at our door. It was always at a time when there was some transition in our lives

Sarafina and the children were all three killed in an automobile crash in 1948. After the accident the managers at Lemonaria sent our mother several boxes of Seraphina's possessions. There was a black stone in the box. It was one of the mirror fragments that Maurilio found many years before. Seraphina had wrapped it and saved it. Maurilio started to dream again after his mother sent him the boxes.

Iuitl tried to teach Maurilio how to control the focus of his dreams, but was not entirely successful. Maurilio became a haunted man after the accident because he felt and still feels that he abandoned his family. Poor Maurilio's dreams since then have mostly been with Sarafina and his children. While he still has dreams of the conquest and the old gods, he cannot focus and has never really been able to clearly see the things that Iuitl was looking for.

.In 1952, we bought the bookstore that Lucinda had worked for. Iuitl gave us some money to complete the purchase. She worked at the store and became quite popular as a story teller and expert on all things about the Mexica and the conquest.

We retired and sold the bookstore in 1981. There were times when we wanted to move into a nicer apartment but Iuitl told us we needed to stay here. She paid most of our expenses; we never knew or asked where she got the money. After we retired, people came here and asked for her to lecture or tell stories to groups. When she went to these groups, her stories became more and more controversial. She told people that the apparition of Guadalupe was faked and that the real Holy mother was an Indian girl who appeared to the Mexica ten years before the supposed appearance of Guadalupe. These stories offended many people. Her interpretation of the conquest and the Mexica were much different than what we have all been taught. This also offended many people. She was taunted, laughed at and called a witch. So, before too long if a group invited her, she would go, but she would speak Nahuatl only. It was at this time that she stopped speaking Spanish. When people in her groups complained, she would become angry and not so nice. Soon word got around and people stopped inviting her.

So now you have come to us with news that you have been dreaming. She was quite excited when she recognized you. I think she will be back soon. She will want to talk with you, hopefully in Spanish.

Stephen looked up and said, "This has been a lot of information and a lot of crazy thoughts that I just don't understand. I need to take one of my pills and go back to the hotel. I suppose I really need to talk with Iuitl. Please don't be offended, but it sounds like she may be crazy, I'm really not sure what to do next."

Martin nodded and looked intently at Stephen and said, "You should talk to her, I think she will be back soon. Don't worry I will call the hotel when she arrives. Now go get some sleep and relax. Let me call a cab driver I know, it's not safe to ride the street cabs at night. Do you want another beer while we wait?"

"No thank you" said Stephen, "no more beer. But maybe we can talk about something else. When I was first here I was writing an article about the recent election. What do you think? Was the election stolen from Cardenas?"

Martin laughed and said, "That's a safe topic, no mystery there. The answer is yes, of course, the PRI would never allow him to be President after he so publically broke away from them."

They sat and talked and laughed for about ten minutes until the cab driver came to the door. Stephen got up and thanked Martin for the beer and the story. He said to remember him to Maurilio and he walked out the door, not understanding much more about Iuitl and his dreams than he had when he arrived. Martin followed him out to the street. As Stephen was about to get into the cab, Martin touched his shoulder and said, "I know this is all very confusing and unbelievable, but come back tomorrow morning and Maurilio may be able to help you understand". Stephen turned and looked closely at Martin, "Ok", he said, "see you tomorrow, good night and thank you Martin."

When he returned to the Hotel, he picked up his bag and went to check in. The girl at the front desk looked his reservation and handed him an envelope. "Senor, there are several phone messages for you here and our manager says that he needs to see you before we check you in". She excused herself and went into the back office. A few seconds later, a tall, well dressed and well-groomed man who looked about thirty years old, walked out and greeted Stephen. With a worried look on his face he held out his hand and invited Stephen to his office. They exchanged the usual pleasantries. He asked Stephen to please sit down. He stared down at his desk for a few moments and then looking up at Stephen with a very pained expression, he said, "You have stayed with us many times and you are a valued guest. Today we have received several phone calls from your wife, Senor. She says that you have had a nervous breakdown and are very ill. She is very worried Senor. She has arranged for us to send you to a doctor here in Polanco. I hate to intrude on your privacy Senor, but please tell me, are you well?" Stephen nodded and smiled, "I am sorry you are involved in this. I am well. You see..." he hesitated for a moment and looked out the window, "you see I needed to come back to Mexico to see a woman. As a man I am sure you understand this. If my wife calls again please tell her I am not here". Stephen took a thousand peso bank note from his wallet and handed it to the Manager. "This should cover the hotels expenses for helping me." The Manager stood up, "Thank you Senor, I understand completely and don't worry, your privacy shall be our priority". They shook hands and Stephen returned to the front desk. He checked in and went to his room on the 34th floor. He sat down to relax and open the envelope. Joice's messages were short and intense. She was very worried; she wanted him to call; she needed to call her right away; she may jump on a plane and come there to get him; she had arranged for a doctor to see him. He felt guilty that for putting her though this.

As he sat there and thought, the hotel phone rang. It was Joice. The sound of Joice weeping on the phone had made one of the girls at the hotel switchboard decide that she would ignore the manager and put the call through.

"Thank god you are Ok. Why did you leave like that? What were you thinking? I have been worried sick..." She went on and on, finally Stephen stopped her. "STOP", he said, "Let me talk. First of all, you told me to leave, don't you remember", she tried to interrupt and Stephen spoke over her. "I have some things I need to settle here. I will explain when I get home. The dreams have stopped, the medication is working. I am fine. I have gotten myself involved with some people who have a fascinating story to tell. This is my work Joice. Finding stories like this and writing about them. Listen I need to sleep. I will call you tomorrow. If I have problems I promise I will see the doctor you found. Now don't worry. I love you and we will talk tomorrow." Joice was calmer and she said "All right, sleep well. I'll worry, but as long as you keep your promise and go see the doctor if the dreams come back, I'm ok. I love you, sleep well". She hung up the phone.

He sat there in the room and looked outside, shook his head, undressed and went to bed. It was the first night in several weeks that he slept soundly and did not dream.

The phone rang at seven thirty. Stephen picked up the phone, not quite awake. It was Martin. "Iuitl has just arrived; she needs to see you right away. Please come as soon as you can". Stephen listened and mumbled in reply, "Yes, give me about an hour".

By eight twenty five he was knocking at Martin's door. Iuitl opened the door and stood there without speaking, looking at him very closely. Martin appeared and said, "Where are your manners? Invite him in". Iuitl nodded and motioned with her hand for Stephen to come in. Martin told Stephen to sit down at the table and asked if he wanted coffee or perhaps something stronger. Iuitl still stood at the doorway watching him. "Yes, I'll have some coffee. Just leave it black, no cream or sugar". He sat down. He looked back at Iuitl and said "Cualli cemihuitl". This was a Nahuatl phrase that he had looked up and memorized for when he would meet her again. He thought it meant good day. She laughed and said in Spanish, "your Nahuatl is not so good. We can speak Spanish". Stephen smiled, "yes that would be better, but I thought you did not like to speak Spanish". "We need to communicate", she said, "I am sorry I do not speak English. We have many things to talk about and I have a task I need you to help me with. I can pay you so well that you will never need to work again". Stephen looked at her closely. She did not look like someone with lots of money. Martin returned with two cups of coffee and one very fragrant cup of unsweetened coco on a tray. He sat the tray on the table. He took the coco and put it in front of the chair that Iuitl was moving towards. Martin sat, Iuitl sat, and she began to speak. "Martin has told me about your troubles, your dreams, and I believe that he told you about what happened to Maurilio. Have you ever read the book *One Hundred Years of Solitude* written by Gabriel Garcia Marquez?" Stephen replied, "Yes, I have read it twice". "Good", she continued, "There is a passage about dreaming, *"....try to find your hands while you are dreaming. If you can see your hands, you can exist in your dreams. You can wander your dreamland at will."* "You see, our normal dreaming is like trying to read a book when all the pages have been jumbled and turned every which way, This kind of dreaming makes no sense. I need to teach you too control your dreams and write them down. I will pay for what you write. It is very important to me and time is running out." Stephen stroked his chin, looked at her and answered, "This all sounds very interesting. I need to tell you, however, that I don't really believe all this new age mysticism. I'm a very practical down to earth person. But I'll listen and try to understand. Especially if it helps me sleep again without all the medicine I'm taking. By the way where is Maurilio?" Martin spoke, "He is asleep. He sleeps late".

Iuitl began to talk again "Good, I know you can do this, because, well, because it has already started. Don't be afraid or think I am insane. But I have seen you in your dreams, and I think you have seen me. That's why I know that you can help me. Let's get started. Martin told me that you have a piece of the mirror?" Stephen answered, "Yes I have a piece of something". Iuitl quickly said, "It is piece of an obsidian mirror that was broken a few months before the final destruction of Tenochtitlan. For thousands of years mirrors made of various materials and were used as portals in time by all of the Mesoamerican cultures. It seems that some people are more sensitive to the mirrors than others. The dreams you are having are triggered by the mirrors. You read Tomas's writings and the mirrors organized your dreams based on thoughts and perhaps repressed memories of past lives. I really don't know how it works. The old gods still have some power. But regardless I suppose it doesn't matter why or how. What really matters is that I teach you to "see your hands" as Marquez says. To do what I need you to

205

do, you must be able to put your dream self in specific places and specific times. Do you have the fragment that you found?" Stephen was truly bewildered with all this; he sat there trying to take it all in. After a minute or so, he shook his head and said, "I left the fragment at home, I didn't bring it." He then remembered that he had not dreamed since he left home. Maybe he thought it wasn't the pills he was taking; maybe the fragment really did cause the dreams. Iuitl looked at him and said, "We have several fragments. Some are here on my sash. Maurilio has one. But we have found that the power of each fragment is attached to a specific person. Probably mine or Maurilio's will not work for you. It would take weeks for yours to be mailed to us. Perhaps we could go to your home and get it. There is not much time left." Then Martin spoke, "Esteban you mentioned a dog collar. You said you got your fragment from a dog's collar. What kind of dog was it? Where did you ...?." Iuitl interrupted him," A dog? What kind of dog? I need to know where this dog is". Stephen spoke again, "The dog and his owner went in a door just a few buildings down the street. It seemed like the dog wanted me to find the fragment. He scratched it off his collar and then kept looking at me as he walked off."

Stephen could tell by her expression that this puzzled Iuitl. There was a noise in the hallway and Maurilio came walking into the room. "I've been listening", he said. "I know the dog and I know his companion her name is Esmerelda. She looks and acts like I imagine the whore, Florida, in Tomas's book would look and act." Stephen excitedly said, "Florida, Florida and the dog, they were in Tomas's book. Don't you remember?" Iuitl nodded and said, "Yes of course we remember them. Florida died but her dog saved my life. I don't understand why this dog we are talking about would have pieces of mirror and why it would be here?" Stephen broke in again, "A dog saved your life? A dog saved Tomas's wife's life." Iuitl sighed and raised her eyebrows, looking at Maurilio and Martin. There was a very uneasy silence in the room; finally Maurilio spoke again, "I have talked to Esmerelda about it. She thinks I am crazy. She says she knows nothing about any of this. But the dog, the dog is very odd, almost like he understands everything that is said." Iuitl nodded and said, "Yes, now we should go and see this Esmerelda and her dog"

Part 6 Esmerelda

They knocked at the door Maurilio pointed out to them.
There was a deep growling and barking from inside. Maurilio
shouted though the closed door, "Esmerelda, it is me, your
neighbor Maurilio Saldivar, open up." "Go away, I'm busy,
I'm working. I can't come to the door, go away". Iuitl
answered loudly, "Please talk to us; I'll give you a thousand
pesos, Just talk to us". The dog stopped barking and
growling. There was a commotion inside. Florida was cursing
and a male voice was yelling. After a minute or two, there
was a crash, the male voice cried out in pain. The door
opened and a man came running out pulling on his pants.
His face was bleeding and he was cursing and yelling as he
ran. Esmerelda came to the door dressed in a pink and
purple flowered fleece robe. She looked at Iuitl and said "Let
me see the money. Who are you?" Iuitl pulled the money
from her sash and held it out. "Let's sit down and talk".
Esmerelda looked at the money and looked at the four of
them standing there and said harshly, "If you want me to do
all four of you, it will be more money, at least two thousand
pesos. Maybe more for the old fool Maurilio. He would
probably have a heart attack. Only three customers died
here in the last ten years. The mordida[34] for the police is

---

[34] A bribe

expensive. I don't want him to die here. If he does, you will need to carry him off." Maurilio looked offended. Iuitl said "We want only to talk. Please invite us in." Esmerelda moved back from the door and motioned for them to come in.

When they were all in and seated, Iuitl began. "Who are you Esmerelda? Are you dreaming?" Esmerelda looked puzzled, then a little angry. She lit a cigarette and coughed a heavy smoker's cough and said, "What is this? Are you some kind of social worker? I am who I am. My only dreams are of painfully dismembering my customers and feeding them to my dog Tezca." It was Iuitl turn to look puzzled, she said. "Then tell us about the dog. How long have you had him? Where did you get him? Why did you name him Tezca?" The dog barked once and walked over to Iuitl and lay at her feet. Esmerelda was surprised by this. "You are asking all these questions. If you are the police, tell me now and I'll pay you and you can leave. Why are you asking these stupid questions?" Iuitl held out the money again and said, "We mean you no harm. We are not police or social workers. My friend here", She pointed to Stephen, "is a writer and he is working on a book. You may become famous. We will pay you more when the book is published." Esmerelda was suspicious, but she said, "All right. I'll answer, Only 10 minutes more. I have another client coming and he won't want anyone to see him. As for Tezca, he is an odd dog. He comes and goes. I don't know where he goes, but sometimes he is gone for weeks. When he is here he protects me. When I first found him I was walking in the Zocolo[35], it was about four years ago. He followed me home. I would not let him in. He sat outside for days. Whenever I went out he followed me. One day a client's wife met me on the street and threatened me with a gun. I, of course, had my knife, and when I pulled it out, she pointed the gun at me and was ready to shoot. Tezca jumped at her and knocked the gun away. I beat her and took the gun. I still have it, but I prefer my knife when there is trouble. After that I let Tezca in. He sniffs the clients when they arrive and growls a little. No one bothers me anymore. Even the police are more respectful. His name came when we were walking between the Templo Mayor and the Cathedral. A street boy was selling black light posters. Tezca stood at one of them and whined, looking at me and looking at the poster. It was a picture of spirit creature, some kind of half animal and half man. Tezca would not leave and I finally bought the poster. When I brought it home and unrolled it, I found the name Tezcatlipoca. It was a powerful Aztec god. It was then that I named the dog Tezca."

The dog looked up at Iuitl and barked once. Iuitl reached down and looked closely at the dog's collar. "Where did these stones come from?" The dog stood up and circled three

---

[35] The central square in Mexico City. The Grand Temple, the Templo Mayor of the Mexica occupied part of the area the Zocolo is in now.

times, than sat again. "The stones, are they valuable? Is this what all your questions are about? They are mine I found them in an old place I lived near here. They were under a loose floor board." Maurilio interrupted her, "Ha, those stones, I put them there back in 1913". Esmerelda continued, "You're crazy old man. They are mine. On the day we moved in there, Tezca was sniffing around and started to dig at the floor. I moved him away and found the board was loose. When I pulled it up I found these stones. They are obsidian. Tezca would not leave them alone. Wherever I put them he would stand and whine. I laid them on the floor and he curled up around them. I decided to have a collar made for him and I took them to a friend who glued them on a leather collar. They shine and sparkle. Even in the dark they glow."

Iuitl said, "Thank you. I want my friend Stephen to touch the collar. Stephen come here and touch it." Before Stephen could get up Tezca walked over to him and scratched at the collar with his rear leg. A stone fell off. Esmerelda began to get up to get it. Stephen reached down and picked it up and it began to glow brighter than before. Iuitl stood up. "We wish to buy this stone. How much do you want?" she said. Esmerelda replied, "Tezca loves these stones. Why would you want them? He lost one a few weeks ago. And now I remember, your friend here, the writer, I ran into him on the day Tezca lost the other stone. What's going on?" Iuitl held up her sash, "I have stones just like it on my sash. I'll give you two of them and two thousand pesos for the ones that fell off the collar." Martin and Maurilio were used to Iuitl spending lots of money, but this shocked them. Esmerelda was suspicious. She walked over and looked at Iuitl's sash. She never sold or bought anything without bargaining. "Ok", she said. "if you want it so bad. Give me two stones and three thousand". Iuitl pulled more money out and handed it to Esmerelda. Esmerelda was still suspicious and said, "If you are cheating me, you will be sorry. I have many friends, police, judges, gangsters. You'll be sorry" The dog walked over to Esmerelda and growled. She was taken aback by this, the dog had never growled at her before. Iuitl stood up and told Stephen to put the stone in his pocket. She thanked Esmerelda and they all stood up and walked out the door. They could hear the dog panting hard as they left.

When they got out on to the street, Stephen said to Iuitl, "I don't mean to be rude and I know it's none of my business, but where do you get all this money. You don't seem to work". Iuitl stopped and looked at him, "The Mexica hid treasure in many places, gold, silver and other valuable things. Remember who I am Stephen. You and everything here are a dream. Please say no more about it." Stephen was taken aback by this, and stopped talking.

Part 7 The Dreamer

The first dream

They walked silently back to Calle Mina. They went into the
courtyard and Martin unlocked the door. Stephen walked in
behind Iuitl and said, "Now what?" Iuitl turned and told him
that he only needed one more thing and then she would give
him some instructions and he could get to work. She told
him to wait and she walked down the hall. Martin and
Maurilio smiled at him and asked if he needed a drink. The
three men stood there not speaking, looking at each other.
Soon Iuitl came back carrying a leather bag. "These are
psilocybin mushrooms. You will need to eat one before you
start.' She handed him one. "After you eat it, we have
prepared a dark place for you to sleep. We will make sure no
one can interrupt you. The stone will be beside you, think of
Tomas, and think of the last sentence in the book. Look into
the stone. Try not to let other thoughts come into your brain.
If you don't concentrate your dreams will continue to be a
jumbled chaotic mess. The most important thing to
remember is to keep your concentration, don't let your
thoughts stray. Think only of Tomas. Soon you will sleep and
dream. Once you are dreaming look at your arms and hands
and then practice walking to your right, then turn and walk
to your left. Learn to control your movement. There will be
other people around you. They won't be able to see you. Look

213

for Tomas. He will be taller than most of the Mexica. His beard will be full. I think you will recognize him. Find him and follow him for as long as you can. Dream time is different; even if you sleep just an hour sometimes your dream can last months or even years and sometimes they last only a few hours. Remember what you see so you can tell me about it and we can finish Tomas' story". Stephen looked at the mushroom and then at Iuitl. "Why can't YOU do this? You seem to be able to control these dreams." Iuitl answered, "A person cannot dream of a time or place where they are alive. I don't know why, it just doesn't work." Stephen shrugged and nodded, "Ok I'll try it. I took a lot of psychedelic drugs back in the sixties. I'm not sure I can control my thoughts. What if I freak out?" Iuitl said, "You will need to stay here. I have cleaned and prepared Martins room. If you get into trouble, we will be here to take care of you. Don't worry. Try to stay focused".

By now Stephen had lost most of his suspicions about being robbed or swindled. He had decided he would write the whole experience as a feature article. He wanted to go back to the hotel to make notes. He was not sure he wanted to take a psychedelic drug like this here, where no one other than these three odd people knew where he was. He told Iuitl that he would go back to the hotel and do it. She told him that she thought doing that was a mistake. "Just remember," she said, "no one will be there to help you if the dreams get out of control. It might be dangerous."

After telling her that he thought he would be ok, Iuitl looked over at Martin and nodded to him. Stephen felt a sharp sting in his shoulder; he jerked around and saw that Martin had injected him with a hypodermic needle. He began to panic. "What are you doing?", he yelled. Then his legs buckled and he found himself on the floor, not quite sure where or who he was. Iuitl looked at him and said, "I regret we had to do that. But if you panic, you will be glad we are here with you."

Martin and Maurilio helped him up and led him into a room down the hall. He lay down on the bed. They took off his shoes and covered him with a light blanket. Iuitl lifted up his head and held the mushroom to his mouth. "Eat this she said, you will see amazing things very soon." He mumbled something and then ate the mushroom. Maurilio gave him some water and Martin reached into his pocket and pulled out the stone. Iuitl laid his head down and held the stone in front of his eyes. The stone glowed. Martin began to read from the final passages in Tomas's book.

Stephen could faintly hear Martin reading, he tried to open his eyes and all he could see was fuzzy and gray light. There was a murmur coming from someplace nearby. Martin's voice was disappearing. The murmur was starting to sound like voices, hundreds of voices. There were lights, like firefly's coming closer and growing bigger. He could see faint shadows of people running about and shouting. It was night. The only light was the lights of torches and bonfires with flames dancing high into the sky. He was standing next to a stone wall or some kind of structure. There were stairs leading up, stairs with narrow treads and very high raisers. He took a step and started to fall. As he fell he looked down and saw his hands and arms. He tried to catch himself but seemed to be tumbling over and over through the air. He suddenly remembered what was happening. This was a dream, either that, he thought, or Iuitl had drugged him or he was hallucinating. He willed himself to stop tumbling and to anchor his feet on the ground. The people all around had weapons, spears and clubs. They were like an angry mob, yelling and shouting. He started to crawl up the stairs to get away from the people. No one seemed to notice him. He crawled for what seemed like a long time. He finally came to platform where there were torches and fires. Figures with long matted hair and dressed in black were chanting and dancing. He could see four other figures in the background. They were dressed like pictures he seen of old Spanish conquistadors. He looked to the right and there was another of the Spaniards lying backwards over a low stone table. One of the men in black plunged a shiny dagger into this man's chest, the man screamed as his murderer pulled the still beating heart out of his chest and held it high above his head for the people below to see. Blood spurted everywhere. The man in black kicked the dying man down the side of the building. The noise level from the crowd below increased by what seemed like tenfold. Another of the conquistadors was being pulled by his hair to the table or altar. Stephen stood up and yelled, "STOP, STOP for god's sake STOP!" No one paid any attention to him. He remembered that Iuitl had said that no one could see him. He ran to the man with the dagger and tried to shove him away. Nothing happened Stephen had no substance. His hands moved through the man's body like nothing was there. A movement in the air above caught his attention, he looked up. He saw dark shadows in the smoke swirling, faces and bodies began to form. They were huge, horrible man animals like nothing he had ever seen. At this point Stephen lost control. All he could do was stand there and scream.

Someone was touching him, shaking his shoulder. He was lying in a bed. He opened his eyes. There were two figures standing in front of a dim light. Martin was looking down at him. Martin's face was glowing like a black light poster. Iuitl was standing there beside Martin. She was glowing also and had a rose colored ring around her body. She was chanting and praying. She looked down at Stephen and said, "It's ok. We took the stone away, Sleep now and later we can talk about it. Don't worry you're safe and you won't dream this time when you close your eyes." He lay there, looking back and forth at them. He could not speak and he was afraid to close his eyes. Iuitl touched his forehead and bent over and looked at him with her deep brown eyes. Stephen looked up and into her eyes. He could see the sky in her eyes. There were stars, uncountable stars. She said, "it's over, sleep now, sleep a dreamless sleep". She put her hands over his eyes.

Stephen awoke smelling coffee and fresh tortillas de harina cooking. He sat up and looked around, slowly remembering where he was and what had happened. He stood and walked out of the room and down the hall. He looked into one of the rooms, it was a small kitchen. Iuitl was standing there making the tortillas. "I thought I heard you wake. Go to the table. I'll bring you coffee and tortillas. I will be there in a minute." Stephen mumbled, "good morning", and continued to the front room and the table. Martin sat there drinking coffee and reading a newspaper. He looked up and smiled at Stephen. "Sit down, you must be very tired and probably a little shaken. When Iuitl comes in you can tell us all about it. Stephen sat and asked where Maurilio was. Martin answered, "He is still sleeping. He is also very tired. We think he may have been with you last night". Iuitl walked in. She had a tray of coffee, butter, and a stack of warm tortillas. She sat the tray down and served the two men. She then sat, took a sip of the coffee and said," Tell us where you were and what happened. "Stephen looked at them, took a sip of his coffee grimaced a little and said, "Whew that's a lot of sugar, can I get black coffee?" Iuitl looked at him and impatiently said, "Yes, yes, yes I will get black coffee for you, but first tell us what happened."

Stephen told them the dream. He shuttered a bit as he told it. The memory of the dream was more clear and alive than any other dream he had ever had. When he got to the final part, where the clouds and smoke was forming faces and grotesque creatures, Iuitl stopped him and explained what he saw, "For the people who were present, these were illusions, I believe you call it "smoke and mirrors". But the old gods are real. You as a dreamer and some of the priests or bloodmen, as Tomas called, them can actually see the real manifestation of these beings. But now, concentrate on what else you saw." And then she stood up and walked back down the hall. Stephen looked at Martin. "She has been waiting for you for a long time." Martin said. "I wish I could do it. I wish I could see all you have and will be seeing. But all the same it sounds terrifying." Stephen started to speak but Iuitl walked back to the room with another cup of coffee. She handed it to Stephen and shook her head, "Black is an unhealthy color, but here it is." She also carried a three ring binder that she laid on the table and opened. She pulled out pages of drawing and pictures. "Did the faces that you saw look like any of these?" she asked. "Well I guess a little", he held one up and turned it sideways, "this one for sure" he said. She took it from him and looked at it. "Tezcatlipoca, it has always hated me because I learned the power of the mirrors. You will need to be careful." This comment frightened Stephen. "You said that no one could see me. Can this thing see me?" She answered, "It is one of the old gods. They live outside time. And yes they see you. But they hurt you only if you let them. The idea that they drink blood is an evil thought they have put into people minds to create what these demons really thrive on; fear, greed, cruelty and hatred. They will try to scare you and tempt you, but if you see them, just laugh at them. Remember we are beings who live in a time-bound world, everything you see has already happened. Don't be afraid or think you can change anything. Try to imagine that it's a three dimensional history book that you are reading." For several moments Stephen looked at Iuitl, turning what she had said over in his mind. He took a big sip of the coffee and nearly choked. "Wow this is strong." Iuitl shrugged, "you wanted it black".

They sat at the table without speaking and drank their coffee. Stephen shrugged again and began to talk," I saw a sacrifice, Spanish soldiers I suppose. It was horrible". Iuitl changed the mood and the conversation. She said she wanted to know about Stephen and his family and how he felt about religion and the world in general. She said that he had heard all of their stories and now he must tell them his. So he began to talk about his wife, his family, his dog, his property in Oregon. But after about ten minutes he stood up and said" I need to get some air, I need to walk around. He put his hand in his pocket looking for his pills. "The anti-anxiety pills I had, they're gone." Iuitl said, "Yes we took them, they will interfere with your dreams. When you're done we will give them back, if you want them. Let's go outside for a while". Stephen was not too happy about this, but accepted it. He told them that sometime today he needed to go back to the hotel to change clothes, shower and call his wife. Martin agreed and said "Sure, let's walk and we can call you a taxi later." The three of them, Maurilio was still in his room asleep, walked out onto the street. Martin suggested that they go to the Zocolo and walk around the Templo Mayor[36].

They walked the four or five blocks to the center of the city where the temple was being excavated. They navigated through the usual crowd of street vendors, snake charmers and con men who were always there. They paid the one hundred peso admission fee and walked past the fence and gate house onto the path around the Templo Mayor. Iuitl pointed out the places where Alvarado and his men had committed the massacre that revived the old gods and human sacrifice. She told them all about how the city had

---

[36] The ruins of the main Mexica Temple- Hueteocalli- adjacent to the main square (Zocolo) in downtown Mexico City.

been laid out around the temple and about what was still covered by streets and buildings. After a half hour or so of walking around and listening to Iuitl, Stephen said he needed to sit down. Iuitl pulled a bottle of a dark liquid from her sash and handed it to Stephen. "Drink this. It's an energy drink I made."

Stephen took a drink from the bottle. It was sweet but had an underlying bitterness.

Within minutes Stephen began to feel dizzy and very relaxed. People's faces began to change and seem somehow distorted. The sky and clouds were full of color and sounds of the street became music of a sort. Stephen sat down on a nearly bench. "You've dosed me with a psilocybin again haven't you". They nodded and Iuitl said, "you need to get back to work I don't have much time, we need to finish". She took him by the hand and they walked out of the Templo area onto the street. Martin hailed a cab and they went back to the rooms on Calle Mina.

Stephen fell asleep during the 4 minute cab ride. When they got to Calle Mina, Iuitl and Martin had to lift him out and help him walk to the room where he had dreamed during the previous night. Stephen was asking for Joice and mumbling about seeing her.

Iuitl looked at Martin and said, "We need to get his mind off his wife. He will wind up like Maurilio. "Is there a picture of her in his wallet?" They took his wallet and looked through it. There was a photo of Joice dressed in an evening dress with Stephen in a tuxedo by her side. Iuitl examined it. "The face is so small, but I'll try. Get that glass mirror in the bathroom" she said. Martin left and quickly returned with the mirror. He handed it to Iuitl. She shook Stephen, and held the mirror in front of his eyes, while Martin held the photo in back and above his head so that it reflected back into the mirror. "Joice is here Stephen; she is holding your hand. She wants you find Tomas. Think of Tomas and find him. Joice will be here when you return". Stephen opened his eyes and stared at the mirror. Iuitl took his hand. He closed his eyes.

The second dream

The experience of dreaming started the same way as it had before. The gray fog in his mind gradually cleared, the place he was standing gradually took shape. The sounds he could hear slowly went from being a dull din to being distinct voices and noises of carts being pulled. There was rain falling all around him, but he could not feel it. He was standing in a street beside a building. The wall next to where he was standing had a smooth finish but as he looked up he could see it was sculpted into intricately carved and brightly painted geometric patterns with faces and animal like beings intermingled.

It was night but there were many fires and torches lit on the neighboring buildings and in the street. On the other side of the narrow street he was standing in, there was a canal. He could hear the rain pouring into the water form gutters on the buildings around him. There were voices nearby that began to sound distinct and clear. He looked down and could see his hands. He tried walking. Everything seemed to be working. He heard noises behind him and turned around. There were four people and a large dog leaving the building. They had no torches or lights. They were walking towards him. They all had robes thrown over their bodies and heads. But he got a good look at them as they passed. The larger man had a full beard. Perhaps, he thought, this was Tomas.

The next person was probably Florida, she did indeed look like Esmerelda. The dog walked beside her. It looked like the same dog he had seen in Esmerelda's apartment. The dog stopped and looked up at Stephen and attempted to lick his hands. The third person was a young Indian man; this, he thought, was possibly Ocelotl. Then to his surprise he saw that Iuitl was the fourth person. She looked at him as they passed. She stopped, made some motions with her hands and said something in Nahuatl. He said her name and asked if she could hear him. She turned quickly and continued walking but kept looking back. They walked single file and stayed close to the buildings until they got to a ramp the led down to the canal. There was a man in large canoe waiting in the water. They all got in the boat. Stephen, not knowing quite what to do, jumped in also. He had no weight or substance so the boat did not rock or move as he got in. He sat in the front so he could watch. Iuitl avoided looking at him. He could see Tomas talking to her and she shook her head as if saying no to him. They all began to row.

Tenochtitlan was a city of canals, much like Venice. The canals formed the transportation system of the city. The work of the city did not shut down at night, many canoes loaded with food and other goods paddled through the canals to their destinations. Stephen looked around at the amazing sights of the city at night. The huge pyramid shaped temples had fires burning from the top that served as tall beacons.

The shadows cast from these fires and the other torches and fires along the canal and in the buildings of the city made everything seem alive and in constant motion and change. The shapes of buildings, people, canoes and everything he saw became alternately elongated and shortened, widened and thinned. Stephen thought that he should try to leave the canoe and climb or maybe even try to fly up to one of the temples so he could see more. But suddenly the city was alive with drums and horns and shouting from all sides.

The canoe turned left on to the larger main canal. As they turned, Stephen saw flashes and shadows of hundreds of people and carts running towards the causeway that led to Tlacopan[37]. He could hear the hooves of horses being ridden on the stone streets. He knew it was the Spanish. Perhaps this was the night they escaped from the city, the event known as La Noche Triste, the Night of Sorrow. It was the night the Spanish escaped from the city. About half of them died and they lost most of the treasure they had stolen. Tomas and the others in the canoe became quite excited and agitated when they saw the Spanish escaping. They were all talking at once. The oars all went to one side and the boat began to turn around. But as they looked in the direction they were turning to, Stephen and the others saw hundreds, maybe thousands of people, some in canoes and some

---

[37] A City allied to the Mexica across the lake from Tenochtitlan

running along the streets towards them. The rain began to fall harder. The canoe turned again and rowed fast towards the Spanish. "Great", Stephen thought, here I am dreaming some kind of psychedelic dream in a canoe between two armies in what will turn out to be a awful, bloody battle. He thought he should wake himself up before things got worse. The boat was moving very fast. Arrows began to fly overhead from the back and gunfire was coming from the front. He could see fires burning on the roof tops in front. People were on the roofs throwing stones and spears at the Spanish. Soon the Spanish would arrive at the beginning of the Tlacopan causeway, one of the bridges across the lake. Stephen could tell that Tomas and the others in the canoe had thought about going down a side canal, but every time they came to an intersection and began to turn they saw that there were warriors and people coming towards them, so they continued rowing towards the Spanish. A movement in the water caught his eye; he looked down and saw the first bodies floating in the water. They were Indian warriors maybe Tlaxcalan, maybe Mexica, he could not tell.

Stephen had never really considered what a battle at night consistent light. The chaos of a pitched battle at night with the only light coming from fires on the tops of buildings and torches being carried by running people was a surreal and disorienting experience. He watched the jerky motion of the people and the flashing of swords and obsidian tipped

227

spears. This moving, living light along with the splashing and thudding of thrown stones, the screams of the wounded and the war cries of the battle was making him somewhat nauseous. All this was happening in a hard rain, with fires and smoke, and occasional thunder and distant lightning. It was total chaos.

Now more and more bodies appeared in the water. The canals were not deep and the canoe kept hitting objects that had fallen into the water, he suspected that many of these were the bodies of Spanish weighed down with arms and treasure.

The boat turned again and was being rowed to the side of the canal, up to a small pier like structure with three canoes tied underneath, Stephen saw Tomas and Florida cutting these boats loose and pushing them out into the canal. Soon their canoe was under the pier and away from the fighting. Stephen knew from his past reading how this battle would turn out. There would be two to four hundred Spanish killed along with thousands of Mexica and Tlaxcalans. The Spanish would barely survive. According to the history books most of the treasure that they had looted would remain in the silt at the bottom of the canals.

They could see flashes of the battle continuing along the bridge in front of them. It looked like some of the Spanish were now far ahead. Stephen looked at the people in the boat. The obsidian mirrors on Iuitl's sash glowed and cast a very odd light. It was what Stephen would later describe as a "dark light". It illuminated the space under the pier but beyond that it cast shadows that were darker than whatever light came from the fires in the city and the reflections from the clouds overhead. Tomas seemed to be wounded and bleeding on his right leg. Florida and Iuitl were tending him and wrapping cloth to stop the bleeding. Iuitl kept looking up at Stephen and then looking away again quickly. The Indian who had been in the canoe waiting for them was badly wounded or perhaps dead. Ocelotl was sitting next to Tomas praying. When they finished bandaging Tomas, they all bowed and prayed. Florida and Ocelotl lifted the Indian out of the boat and laid his body on the dock.

The dog was lying in the bottom of the canoe panting heavily. Throughout the battle and the escape he barked and roared and seemed eager to join the fighting. Florida had tried hard to keep him from overturning the canoe. Stephen could see, even in the dark that her skin was glistening, probably from the exertion she made while holding the dog.

As the fighting continued to move away, the voices and sounds of weapons began to merge into one undefined gray sound punctuated by occasional muffled gun shots and screams. The city seemed almost deserted. Everyone was in hiding or had joined the battle. Stephen noticed that was disagreement in the boat as to where they should go. Florida seemed to be speaking Spanish and Iuitl and Tomas were answering her in Spanish. But the accents and archaic words and phrases were almost unintelligible to him. He could make out words here and there. It appeared that Iuitl and Tomas wanted to head across the lake to Texcoco. Florida was against this and may have been saying that the Spanish were going that way and the fighting would continue there. Finally Iuitl and Tomas agreed with her and the boat was untied from the pier and they all began paddling down the canal towards the lake.

It was not an easy trip. The canal was full of bodies floating. Stephen looked ahead and saw a horse partly submerged. The canoe kept hitting rock and other objects below the surface. They were paddling slowly while trying to dodge the objects that they could see. The sky was beginning to brighten. Stephen could see ahead to what he thought was the main body of water on the lake. Stephen wondered how long this dream had lasted. He started to think of Joice and how worried she must be, the scene around him began to dim and he could barely see anything but a gray haze. He remembered that he had to concentrate and try to keep the dream going. He looked down at his hands and focused on the space behind him where Tomas and the others would be. When the dream came back into focus, He saw that they were in open water and headed towards an island that Iuitl was pointing at.

Within minutes the canoe landed at the island and Tomas and the others got out. Florida helped the dog jump out. Stephen got out with them. Iuitl pointed up to some rocks visible in the trees and underbrush ahead. They all began walking towards the rocks, all except Iuitl. She looked at Stephen and held one of her mirrors towards him. It reflected the dark light into his eyes, nearly blinding him. Iuitl began chanting, while watching Stephen. He tried to move away, but she kept the mirror focused on his eyes. The dog turned away from the others and walked back to Stephen trying to lick him again. Iuitl held out her hands as if to push Stephen away. He said her name and asked her if she remembered him. She continued chanting and leaned over putting her hand to the sand and making a line. She then rose up, held out her hands, palms toward Stephen once more, and then turned to catch up with the others. The dog came as if to help Stephen cross the line. The line had formed a dense gray fog around it, as Stephen crossed. He couldn't see where he was going until he felt the dog next to him. He walked beside the dog and soon the air cleared and he saw the others about 100 feet in front of him He and the dog ran to catch up.

They walked along a path up towards the rocky outcropping Iuitl had pointed out. Along the way they passed stone idols on both sides, some were large and some small. Soon they came to a cave. There were several tall monuments, carved like totem poles, outside the entrance. They were covered in glyphs and faces all painted in dark reds and blues. Iuitl led the group as they entered the cave. She held her mirror out with her arms extended. There was a soft gray light emanating from the mirror that illuminated a place where they saw an altar, stone benches and a small pool of water. She sat the mirror on a shelf-like rock. They all drank from the pool, talked among themselves and after a few minutes, they laid down and slept. The dog also drank and then walked back towards the entrance, turned around a few times and curled up to sleep on the ground just inside the cave.

Stephen walked around looking at the various objects and what seemed to be offerings. He touched one of the statues of what may have been a Mexica god. It was made of a bright blue smooth glossy stone. As he touched it, he noticed something moving in a corner of the cave. The light from the mirror did not illuminate that corner. A shadow was all he could see. He walked closer to it, feeling that he was invisible and ethereal in this dream state. But the shadow began walking towards him. He stopped and as it moved closer he could see that it was also a transparent dream like figure. It was the Mexica god whose statue he had touched. He remembered what Iuitl had told him, and he began to laugh at it. This seemed to anger whatever it was and it pointed an obsidian knife towards him. Its hands were dripping what seemed like blood. Stephen stepped back and saw that Iuitl was standing behind him. She walked forward between Stephen and the shadowy god/demon figure. She had taken the mirror from the shelf and held it up in front of her. This further angered the demon. It now focused on Iuitl and pointed the knife at her. Iuitl stood her ground and the creature did not move closer. Looking past the demon, Stephen saw more movement in the back of the cave, slowly the shadows moved into the light and Stephen saw more demons each one dressed in different regalia and all of them various combinations of man and animal. Suddenly a blue light appeared like a smoke ring around Iuitl, Stephen and the sleepers. He looked down and saw that the dog was there, growling. The Blue smoke began to form into a giant serpent with bright phosphorescent feathers. He remembered his first dream back in the hotel room after he had finished the book. The serpent raised its head and spoke to the demons. They retreated back into the cave. The dog jumped over the serpent and chased after the demons. Stephen looked down and saw that Tomas, Florida and Ocelotl continued to sleep. He heard voices. Iuitl was talking to someone or something he could not see. The serpents head was up and looking at Iuitl and whatever she was talking to. There was a noise coming from the back where the demons had gone. Out of the shadows in the back a transparent figure that appeared to be Alvarado walked towards them. The dog was retreating in front of it barking furiously. Iuitl and the serpent turned, and then a bright white light and a dazzling cross appeared where the head of the serpent had been. Alvarado or the shadow of Alvarado stopped. The cross appeared very solid to Stephen. The dog stood next to the cross and continued to bark. Suddenly Alvarado disappeared and the cave was very quiet. The serpent and the blue light were gone. The cross was gone. Iuitl stood looking at Stephen. He could tell that she did not seem to understand who or what he was. She took a deep breath and lay down next to Tomas, who was still sleeping on the floor of the cave. The dog came up to Stephen and licked his hand. This time he actually felt it. He petted the dog on the back and it walked back to its place at the entrance and lay down.

Stephen was perplexed and very tired. What had happened, what did it all mean? Why didn't Iuitl speak to him, she could obviously see him?

He decided it was time to wake up. He had not come close to learning the fate of Tomas, but all he had seen and been through was so intense that he needed to rest, to really rest.

A stream of jumbled images and voices filled his mind and his vision began turning gray and foggy and then dark and black. The next thing he knew he was opening his eyes looking at a wall in the bedroom at Martin and Maurilio's home. He was disoriented; he could not quite understand where he was. He tried to call for Joice but the sound his voice made was scrambled and unclear. More like a cough than a word.

He tried several times more. The door opened and Martin and Iuitl came in. Iuitl had a damp cloth and washed his forehead and face. Martin set the tray of coffee and pastries he had been carrying down on a table next to the bed.

Iuitl looked down at Stephen and said, "Welcome back, sit up and have some coffee. I have kept it black as you said you like it. When you feel ready and awake, tell us where you were and what happened",

Stephen, suddenly aware of where he was, sat up, "What time is it? Actually, what day is it? I have no idea how long I have been here. I need to call my wife she'll be very worried". Martin told him that he had been there for two days now and that it was morning, about five thirty AM. He then said "I talked to your wife last night; we got the number from the hotel manager. You are right she is worried. I told her that you were working on an assignment of great historical importance. I told her you were in no danger and you would call when you were near a phone again. I must admit she was not entirely satisfied. She said that if you did not call in twenty four hours she was going to contact your company's security department. You can call her this morning, but because of the time difference," he stopped talking and smiled a bit", I mean her pacific time and our central time, not the time difference you have been through," he paused again, "anyway, tell us about your dream and soon she will be awake and you can call her".

Stephen reached down for his coffee, picked it up and said," let's go the table in the front room. I need to walk, I still feel wobbly". Iuitl said, "Yes, yes I understand." She picked up the tray and the three of them walked out and down the hall to the table.

When they were settled at the table, Stephen asked about Maurilio. Martin answered, "He has been trying to help you, to be in your dream or assure that you are in his dream. It is confusing, is it not? Regardless he is tired. He awoke a little before you this morning and said that he had been there. He saw the demons and he saw you. He and Iuitl were able to converse a little. "Iuitl interrupted, "He has more experience, more training I guess you could say. He told us where you were." Stephen looked at Iuitl, "You were Tomas's wife! Why didn't you tell me? Why didn't you answer when I said your name? Iuitl looked at him very intensely," I couldn't really see you, except for a few seconds. All I could see was a half formed gray figure. That's why, when you first came to our door, I did not recognize you. You are not yet able to fully put yourself in the dream. You were only partly there. Your mind was not fully focused. But the reality is that you were not where you needed to be. You did not find out what happened to Tomas or where he went. I need to learn what happened to him. I don't have much time left." Stephen put his coffee mug on the table and looked over at her, "You keep saying you don't have much time left. What do you mean?" Iuitl answered, "We stayed in the cave for three days. On the third day Tomas was weak from loss of blood. I went to the mainland with our disciple Ocelotl to find healing medicines and food. When we got to Chapultepec we split up. As I was foraging, Mexica warriors captured me. Ocelotl managed to escape. I was wearing the blue cloak of Ketsalkoatl. They took me to the demon priests of the war god Huitzilopochtli. They recognized me and took me to the dark part of the temple where those who are to be sacrificed are held. It was then that I began dreaming and in my dream I met Martin and Maurilio. It has been fifty years of dream time but a few months of my life in the prison. The mirror that we all have pieces of was next to my cell. When I am awake I can conjure images up to scare the priests. But now I fear that my time is nearly up. I have heard the moans and cry of the priests and guards dying of Cocoliztu, what you call the small pox.

237

Thousands died while I have been imprisoned. Even Cuitlahuac died. I have heard the remaining priests say that their god wants my blood. Soon I will be on the blood altar of Huitzilopochtli. Before I die, I must know if Tomas survived. So ask us questions about what you saw, call your wife, but please dream again and find Tomas."

"I have read about the La Noche Triste. I have images and impressions in my mind, but to actually see how terrible and horrifying it was, it's more than my brain can handle. I don't want to talk about it. But in the cave, the demons, the plumed serpent, the whole thing with the demon that appeared and looked like Alvarado. And the dog, was it dreaming or was it awake? Why did all this happen, what did it all mean?"

Iuitl began to answer, "The old gods, the demons, whatever you want to call them, they were trying to scare you. They did not know what or who you were. They wanted you gone. Perhaps they wanted to whisper in the ear of the blood priests and tell them where we were. I really do not know. They were strong. The hatred of the Mexica and the Spanish was strong that night and the next day. That is what they thrive on, not blood, they thrive on faith and hatred, just as our God and his sons and the holy mother thrive on faith and love. They are opposites. They did not want Tomas to be remembered. They do not want the appearance of the Holy

Mother to be remembered. The faith of Jesus was weak. Hatred coming from the Inquisition and the greed of the conquistadors has taken it over. The new faith of God's son Ketsalkoatl was strong with love. The old gods, the demons had new followers and had no use for Tomas or his disciples.

The serpent was Ketsalkoatl; his strength was stronger than the demons. They searched your soul and found a great hatred in your heart; the one you hated was Alvarado. They wanted you to hate. So they came to us in the guise of your hatred. It was then that I saw Maurilio dreaming and watching. I spoke to him. He took the crucifix he wears and held it up to the Alvarado demon. The cross appeared large and strong and shining. The demon retreated. I believe that they understood then that the faith of Jesus was not all greed and hatred.

Stephen interrupted her, "So what you are saying is that I have gotten myself in the middle of some eternal battle between good and evil?" Iuitl answered, "Remember these beings, both the good and the bad, live outside time. This battle you mentioned is an eternal battle. Even now in the twentieth century you are in the middle of the battle. Evil consumes many of the Jesus people now, just as it did in the fifteenth century." Stephen finished the last of his coffee and took the last bite of a pastry. He looked at Martin and Iuitl and changed the subject, "So you could see Maurilio and talk to him?" Iuitl continued, "Yes. Maurilio has been dreaming now for many years. He has great skill and concentration. But this was one of the few times since I have known him that he has been able to dream of something other than Sarafina and his children. He has never been able to help me find Tomas.

Now as for the dog, you want to know about the dog. I wish I understood the dog more. I am not sure if he is the Mexica god Xolotl or something else. In the mythology of the Americas, Xolotl was the companion of Ketsalkoatl. When Tezcatlipoca killed Ketsalkoatl it is said that the dog accompanied and guided Ketsalkoatl to the mythical land at the end of the eastern sea. Even if this dog is not Xolotl, dogs are special creatures. They can remember previous lives. They can see the demons and they can see dreamers. Dogs also have the capacity of great love and great hatred, just like people. So I don't know if the dog we call Tezca is Xolotl or Negruzco or a reincarnation of Negruzco. And now, do you have other questions? If not go call your wife."

The final Dream

Joice sounded relieved when Stephen called her. He told her that he was feeling good and that the project he was working on was something that could change the way historians sees the conquest of Mexico. He said that he was not sure how much longer he would be gone. But he thought that he was nearing the end. She asked him why he could not call in the evenings and why he had not been to the hotel. He thought for a moment and told her that he was actually seeing history and he needed to take advantage of being in what he called "these special places". He said there were no telephones in the places he was visiting. Stephen and Joice had visited many of the archaeological sites in Mexico and Peru so she assumed that he was working on some newly discovered ruins. She said that she understood and asked why he had not been more direct. He nervously laughed and told her that it was a big secret and he would explain it all when he got home. Then he said he had to go, told her he loved her. She said for him to call again soon and he hung up

Stephen went back into the front room. Iuitl seemed very worried and pale. She told Stephen that he had to get back to work soon. She handed him the Psilocybin. He took it. She began to give him instructions about how and where to focus. Suddenly she began to shake and her skin became pale, all most transparent. She said something was happening and she had to go. She squeezed his hand and said good luck and thank you. She told him to throw the pieces of the obsidian mirror into the ocean when he finished. She turned and hugged Martin and went out the door.

The Psilocybin was starting to take effect. Martin, said "Come on, you need to get into bed quickly". Stephen saw the walls in the hallway began to take on bright colors, the five feet of hallway looked to him like an endless tunnel. But within a minute, Martin got him into the bed. The only light in the room was the dark glow of the mirror fragment. Martin began talking to Stephen about the cave and the need to find Tomas.

Stephen tried to focus, but all he could think about was Iuitl and what had happened to her. His mind was full of colors and voices. Then his mind saw a ghost like image of Maurilio standing in the black beckoning him forward. He followed and soon the black gave way to gray and then to the rocky island in the lake where the cave was. There were Mexica warriors and blood priests dragging something. Stephen walked closer. Maurilio was still by his side. He could see that Maurilio was trying to talk to him but he could not hear anything but a static like sound. Stephen looked down, the Mexica were dragging Tomas. He was bound and unconscious, but seemed to be breathing. His leg wound had opened and was bleeding. One of the blood priest motioned to a warrior and they stopped. The bloodman went to Tomas and wrapped his leg in a cotton bandage. Maurilio spoke and Stephen could hear him. "They don't want to waste the blood". Stephen looked at Maurilio and said, "I can see and hear you. What can we do?" "Only watch and follow." said Maurilio. They heard noise from up near the cave. More warriors were dragging two more bundles. It was Negruzco and Florida, neither seemed to be moving. When these new warriors reached the others, they stopped. Stephen looked at Florida first. She had a large bleeding wound on her head. Her eyes were open. She was dead. The dog had wounds also and even though he was not moving, Stephen and Maurilio could hear a low quiet growl. Maurilio told Stephen that the dog had been drugged. The warriors and the bloodmen loaded Tomas, the dog and the body of Florida into a barge like boat. Stephen and Maurilio followed. When they got out into the lake and were headed for Tenochtitlan, Stephen looked at one of the warriors, his face was covered in scabs and he was vomiting into the water. Maurilio saw this also and said, "Smallpox, I imagine we will see a lot of it when we get to the city". Stephen nodded and said, "I wish there was something we could do for Tomas. Iuitl said you were trained in this dreaming. She can touch things and move things, can you do the same?" Maurilio shook his head, "No Esteban, I cannot".

It took about forty five minutes for the boat to arrive at the Grand Canal and enter the city. The canal was still partly blocked by debris. Many the beautiful buildings had been partly burnt. It looked as if some of them had been hacked at to remove stones and the smooth colored finish was pockmarked and damaged on almost all of them. There were very few people walking the streets and the merchant canoes were nowhere to be scene. It was a drastic change from the city he had seen before. He looked down on one of the avenues they passed and could see a stack of bodies being loaded onto a flat boat. It was the time of death; the small pox epidemic was in full force. He was about to say something to Maurilio and looked around. Maurilio had faded to a gray shadow. Stephen tried to touch him. It was like touching smoke, there was nothing there.

The boat reached the Gate of the sacred plaza of Hueteocalli, the grand temple where the holy Virgin of the Mexica had appeared. The plaza was almost deserted. There was rubbish and garbage strewn everywhere. Stephen could see a line of the blood priests coming towards the boat. The warriors in the boat carried their sick comrade off and laid him on a stone bench outside the plaza wall. The bloodmen coming toward them were carrying wooden sleds. Tomas was awake but Stephen could see he was in great pain. The dog was still drugged. Four of the bloodmen took Florida's body and dragged it into a small building near the plaza. The other bloodmen and the warriors from the boat tied Tomas and the dog to the sleds and began to pull them across the plaza and the then up the steep ramp leading to the top of the temple. Stephen looked around again for Maurilio. Even the shadow was gone, so he followed the priest across the plaza and up the temple. The temple was about two hundred feet high. The Mexica dragging their prisoners were running up. Stephen laughed a little and thought that if his corporal body were actually climbing he would have been left far behind.

When they reached the top, five of them took Tomas into the Sanctuary of the war god Huitzilopochtli. Six others began to untie Negruzco. Stephen went into the sanctuary. They were undressing Tomas and had started to paint his body. He moaned and tried to fight with what little strength he had. One of the bloodmen went back into another room and came out with a cloth that he held on Tomas face. Tomas stopped moving, but Stephen could see that he was still breathing.

Stephen walked outside to see what they were doing to the dog. They had lashed him to a slab that stood upright. They were dressing the dog in the regalia of one of the gods. This was the same ritual preparation that Tomas had described on the night of the Holy Mother. The dog truly looked horrifying. He was still drugged but his legs seemed to be kicking and moving like so many sleeping dogs that Stephen had seen. The rope lashing camouflaged in the clothing they had put on the dog, looked very strong and secure.

From somewhere below there were drums, flutes and whistles playing a rhythmic almost melodic music. Evening was coming; the fires on top of the sanctuary were being lit. Some people were starting to assemble below, but only one hundred or so. Definitely not the thousands that had come on the Holy Night Tomas had described. The priests were dancing and chanting in front of the fires.

There were 3 naked and painted men who appeared to be Spanish tied to poles near the altar. Two of the blood priests were leading Tomas out on to the platform. It was probably the same place where the Virgin Mother had appeared. Tomas was led to two ropes hanging down from the roof of the sanctuary of the war god Huitzilopochtli. The priests tied his wrists to the ropes and he was lifted up in front of one of the fires so that the people watching could see him.

The music seemed to be reaching a climax and then the flutes and whistles stopped with only the drums continuing. One of the priests began dancing by himself at the edge of the temples so that he was in full view to the watchers below.. His chants and yells were loud and the drums were now serving as an accent to his words. Tomas was slowing

246

being let down. Stephen looked up and could see the demons being formed in the smoke above the sanctuary like before. One of the priests must have been prodding the dog. It began barking and roaring.

Tomas reached the ground and he was untied and led to the altar. Stephen felt he had to do something, but remembered his past experience. He was standing next to one of the priests. There was a movement behind him. Stephen turned and saw a very faint ghost like Maurilio standing there. Maurilio pointed the Obsidian knife on the priest's sash and said "Concentrate! You must believe you can take it!" Stephen reached down and took it. His hand could actually hold it. To the priest and others watching it appeared that the knife began to move by itself, they could not see Stephen. The priest was terrified and ran off, the others stopped what they were doing and stared at the knife. The knife seemed to be floating in midair. Stephen looked over and his eyes locked onto the dog's eyes, then he began running towards where Tomas was being held. The dog let out a loud mournful cry and broke away from it ropes. It was suddenly running across the platform passing Stephen. Stephen looked up and saw that Tomas was draped across the altar and the priest was standing above him momentarily immobilized by the sight of the knife and then the dog running towards him. The dog leaped at the priest. The two of them tumbled down the side of the temple. The others continued to stand there slack jawed and in shock, listening to the sound of the priest screaming, the dog roaring and the sickening thud of soft bodies bouncing off the stone steps.

Stephen ran to Tomas and tried to move him from the altar. Tomas was dead. The priest must have plunged the knife into his heart just at the moment that the dog hit him. The drums and music had stopped. The smoke illusions above the temple faded up into the sky. Then two of the painted men who had been waiting to be sacrificed ran up from behind Stephen and took Tomas's body from the Altar. Stephen recognized one of them, it was Ocelotl. The knife Stephen held dropped to floor. His hands became transparent and incorporeal. He could no longer touch or move anything. He looked around for Maurilio but saw nothing. Ocelotl and the other man were carrying Tomas between the Sanctuaries and to the back stairs of the temple. By this time the Mexica on the temple platform had gathered at the edge of the temple looking down trying to see what had happened to the dog and priest. They completely ignored Tomas being carried away. Stephen followed them down the stairs. When they reached the bottom, they walked as fast as they could, carrying the body towards the gate of the sacred precinct. Negruzco came limping up towards them, followed by Mexica warriors. He turned to them and growled, he made a faint run towards them and they turned and ran back to the front of the temple where torches still

248

burned and there was light. When they arrived at the gate, there was a canoe with two rowers waiting for them. They put Tomas in the canoe and were about to row into the canal when Ocelotl whistled. Negruzco came limping up barked at them and walked as best he could back to where Stephen was standing. Ocelotl whistled again, Negruzco did not move. The canoe began moving and disappeared into the dark canal.

Stephen stood there in the dark wondering what to do next. He had gained the answer that Iuitl wanted to hear. Tomas was dead.

Suddenly everything was quiet. Stephen heard Iuitl's very weak voice calling him But he could not tell where the voice came from. The dog began walking in front of Stephen, looking back at him, beckoning him to follow. They walked in the dark about 20 feet to a small building. They went in. there were stairs leading down. The torches were still lit and throwing grotesque shadows around them. Stephen thought he recognized the bright painting and relief sculpture on the walls. He had seen pictures in books and at museums with the same themes. He thought to himself, this is a portal to their symbolic underworld. Negruzco had great difficulty going down the stairs. They finally reached the bottom. He saw Iuitl, painted for sacrifice and laying on a stone bench in a corner. She seemed small and very frail. Negruzco curled up and lay down in front of her. Stephen bent over and tried to lift her up, but whatever substance his hands had had before had vanished. He asked her what he could do. She looked up and said," Maurilio was here he told me what happened. Listen and remember, I won't see you again. Ocelotl has an account of all this hidden in the Vatican Library in Rome. Find it. Maurilio has a short epilogue that was never published. It is in his room. Use these things and use what you have seen and read, tell people what happened. Tell people want it means. Wake up now and throw the stone into the ocean as soon as you can. If you keep it you will become insane." Iuitl opened her eyes wide and sat up. She took Stephens shoulder and shook him, with more strength then he imagined she had. Her voice became stronger. She said "WAKE UP, WAKE UP."

The dream ended abruptly. Stephen found himself in bed staring at the ceiling, he shuttered and closed his eyes, he tried to go back into the dream. But nothing happened, the images he had seen were in his head but he was no longer there. After a few minutes he opened his eyes and sat up. He could hear voices coming from the front room. He stood up and began to walk but soon lost his balance and fell against the door. He heard more voices and Martin came into the room along with Esmerelda. Martin looked at him and said, "So you are awake. There are people here, Esmerelda will help you up. Stay here until I come back." Esmerelda helped him back to the bed. She sat down on the bed and looked at him. "Martin has tried to tell me what you all are doing. I don't believe it. It's all Mierda[38] to me. But you must know your cousin or uncle or whatever he was, Maurilio, he died last night. Tezca led me here and will not leave. I wanted to wake you but Martin insisted that we let you sleep. The police and the undertakers are here talking to Martin. They will be gone soon. Martin said that the woman will all the money is dead also. This place has bad luck. I fed Martin and I will feed you but then I must go." Stephen just looked at her, unbelievingly. He mumbled a little and then looking at the wall said, "Maurilio dead, Iuitl dead. I just saw them".

Martin walked back into the room. Esmerelda got up and said," All right you are crazy people. This morning I made Enchilada Especial de Esmerelda for you both. Martin said you had beer. We will have a proper wake for the old man." She got up and walked out the door. Martin began to speak but they heard Esmerelda yelling at Tezca, "Come on you lazy dog, let go home. I'll cut you some fat from the meat. Come on! Come or do I have to drag you." They heard the dog growl. "All right stay here, you are as crazy as they are. I won't give you any beer in your bowl when we eat. Bueno, stupid dog, stay here." The door slammed and shut and they heard the dog walking down the hall to Maurilio's room.

---

[38] Roughly "Bull Shit"

They continued to listen and soon there was a thud from Tezca lying down. Martin spoke to Stephen," She told you?" "Yes" Stephen answered, "But I can't believe it. They were both there in my dream. Did Iuitl die here also?" Martin rolled his eyes to the side and looked down at the floor," No she died in her own time, not in her dream here. She always said that you can never dream of your own death. When you saw her, was she in a room painted to simulate the Mexica underworld?" Stephen nodded. Martin continued, "She said she had been there for several months. It was nearly fifty years for us, but she was dreaming all the time she was being held. It was what kept her alive all those months. The Mexica priests were a little afraid of her. So they just kept here there. She knew she was about to die and, as far as I know she died. Maurilio told me all about what happened in the dream, about Tomas, about the dog and about Iuitl. He was so proud that at last he had been able to do tell her what she wanted to know. He has been trying for all these years. But he was old and the effort he made killed him. He said he willed you to pick up a knife and try to free Tomas. Is that right?" Stephen nodded. Martin continued," It was a great effort for him. He died happy". Stephen spoke again, "So Iuitl. The whole time you have known her she was a prisoner? That is almost more unbelievable than everything else that has happened. Perhaps I can go back and help her escape." "No Esteban, you cannot. Remember everything you have seen has already happened. You can change nothing.

252

Also understand that she believes in what we call reincarnation. She wanted to know when Tomas died so that she could look for him in their next life. I guess it would help her somehow to know. The important thing now is to tell the story. To expose the conquistadors for what they really were. To show the world and the Mexicans that The Holy Mother did indeed come to Mexico. But not as we have been taught, not as a foreigner from Guadalupe in Spain, not as a symbol for the rapists, slavers and thieves who created the Mestizo race. They lied and told us that the holy mother had come because they came. It is not a coincidence that Guadalupe was the name of Cortez's birth place in Spain. Esteban did you know that there is no written record of the appearance of the Virgin of Guadalupe until the early 1600's? You should read a book, "Guadalupe and Quetzalcoatl" by Jacques Lafaye.

These Conquistador rapists came and created our race and then lied and denied us our true mother. This is the story you need to tell. Go to Rome and find Ocelotl's story. Take the codex to experts. Write so all will understand. Maurilio wrote an epilogue for Tomas's book. I will get for you. It explains what you must do."

Martin opened a drawer nearby and pulled out a few pages written in long hand by Maurilio. "None of the publishers would put this in the book. But now it is yours" Stephen did not know what to say or what to do. He took Maurilio writing and looked at it.

The dog barked from the back room. Stephen looked up and asked, "What about this dog. The dog is one part of all this that I still don't understand. Iuitl tried to explain it, but I am not quite sure if I understood. Do you understand it?" Martin shrugged, "Not really. But this is how I understand what we discussed. Remember I told you that Iuitl thinks time really does not exist, at least as we experience it? She thinks that dogs and most other animals experience time differently. She thinks they remember things from previous lives. This memory is what we call instinct. Animals seem to know things without being taught. That's because of this previous life memory. The dog Tezca or Negruzco has he was called has a very strong of memory of what happened. Perhaps it was the drugs the Mexica used on him or the influence of Iuitl. Who knows why. He was devoted to the whore Florida back in that life he lived. Iuitl thinks that when he was born into this life he searched and searched until he found a woman who was almost identical to the mistress he loved so much. A dog's love is very strong Stephen, stronger than we know. But all that is just speculation. Now I will leave you to read, think about what I have told you and read Maurilio's epilogue." Stephen glanced down at the few pages he had been given. He laid back and began to read.

Part 8 Epilogue

Translators Ending Notes:

According to family histories I have heard and baptismal records I have examined. My ancestor Esteban Saldivar, the priest who adopted Tomas, was part of a group of colonists and soldiers who went, whether by choice or order of the church, to the north. Their stated goal was to spread the word of Christ and convert the Indians. Of course the real goal, for most of the people in this expedition, was to find more gold, silver and slaves.

The Zacateco people they met in the north were not easily conquered and enslaved by the Spanish. There was a rebellion in 1538 and the Spanish were driven out. I believe Esteban must have been a friend to the Indians. He was allowed to stay in the area and marry an Indian woman.

When the Spanish returned a few years later, disease had killed many of the Zacatecos, as it did to all the other native peoples. Esteban was soon arrested by the inquisition and burnt alive.

I, Maurilio Saldivar, am a direct descendant of Esteban. Our family has kept the manuscript of Tomas in our custody for all the years that have gone by since the Indian Ocelotl found it in the ruins of Tenochtitlan.

I am now proud to share the life of Tomas with the world during this time of a new Inquisition in Germany and in other places. I share it in the hope that the lesson that Tomas tried to teach will be heard again and understood by people everywhere. For me, and I think for Tomas, the lesson is most simply that Salvation and Love are available for all of us. The way we know and understand God and the lessons he teaches are not the exclusive property of one culture or one religion. God gives different cultures their own mythologies and lore to help us understand. God's love for us is not conditioned by a requirement that destroys our native cultures and orders the conquered to convert or die.

Venceremos,

Maurilo Saldivar DeLara,
1938, Jerez, Zacatecas

Enchiladas

Stephen finished reading and sat there on the bed in awe of what he was tasked with doing next. He started to think about going to Rome. His AP credentials would help in the job of finding Ocelotl's story and the account of the appearance of the Holy Mother. He was sure that the significance of it was forgotten after so long.

He heard the door of the front room open and then slam shut. Tezca was walking down the hall towards the door. He got up and to the front room. Esmerelda was there, cursing loudly as usual. On the table there were three bottles of Indio beer and a big platter of Enchiladas. They all sat down, said a prayer for Maurilio and Iuitl, and then began to eat. Tezca was lying down again, sleeping in a corner of the room. He made a quiet, high pitched bark and Stephen looked over at him. His eyes were closed but his legs were moving, he was twitching and growling. Stephen smiled, a dogs dream, he thought. Maybe he'll break his bonds a little sooner this time and catch the blood priest before its too late.

END

29934187R00141

Made in the USA
Columbia, SC
25 October 2018